Jack & Amy

Jack has never had a home or parents—he lives with his dog Miter in a shelter he has made. Amy lives in a wealthy mansion house with her uncle, who treats her cruelly. Jack meets Amy in an unusual way and helps her to escape, by means of a white horse they call Daybreak.

Escape is not as easy as it seems, however, and the children are pursued by a rider on a black horse. Amy is stolen away by the Black Rider and Jack makes it his task to rescue her, as well as to find out the meaning of the three chests in the towers in the forest.

A tale of creation, of the White Rider and his dark counterpart, of homes and homelessness; weaving through worlds of fantasy and dream Jack and Amy come to know the true meaning of home.

Beamore Books takes its name from the Beaghmore Stone Circles in County Tyrone, Ireland.

Jack & Amy

Ranald Macdonald

Beamore Books

First published by Beamore Books in 2005

Beamore Books,
61 River View, Kilkenny, Republic of Ireland

Text copyright © 2005 Ranald Macdonald

Ranald Macdonald asserts the moral right to be identified as the author of the work.

British Library CIP Data available

Cover illustration © Beamore Books

Printed in England

ISBN 0 9535589 4 0

Jack & Amy

Chapter One—Homes

Once there was a boy called Jack. He had no parents. He had no home. But he did have a place of his own—in a wooden box. Neither you nor I need to know why he lived on his own—he might have been a runaway, an orphan, a lost boy—but the important thing to know is, he was not lonely. He had a dog called Miter. He did not know where the name came from. But it *was* Miter's proper name.

Jack had dark hair and Miter had dark hair. Jack had bright eyes and Miter had bright eyes. They were a pair, Jack and Miter.

His box was very comfortable. It was dug into a bank in a deserted lane. It opened into a burrow in the ground. The burrow had an upstairs and a downstairs. You had to pull yourself up to get into the second room, the upstairs one. It had a sheepskin in it and a bundle of woolly fleece Jack had collected from fences. There was moss and dry grass. The rain *never* came in. It was so warm you would not know if the snow lay thick outside. Miter loved it with Jack, and curled up beside him every night, quite contentedly.

Jack never knew how old he was. About your age, perhaps. But as he lived so much outdoors, and was friends with the sun, moon and stars, he had his own idea of time. If he felt like being out at night, he would stay out for as long as he wanted. If he felt like sleeping in the day, he would do that. He slept for a week in winter once, when the weather was bad—just curled up there in his burrow, like a hedgehog hibernating.

He had no idea of money. If he needed food or clothes he went rummaging in people's rubbish bins. Now you must understand he was a tidy boy, a clean boy, and perfectly harmless. He was rather like a fox who knows where to find good things. People there had *very* well stocked rubbish bins. Jack knew just where to look for the best food and drink and clothes.

You might wonder how it was possible for a boy to live in a burrow like that without being caught and put in a home. The answer is that people there did not speak to each other. They did not need to. It was a very rich area, of leafy lanes and high walls. If someone did come to a house, he would have to speak through an intercom at the gate. That was how Jack got to know Amy.

Amy

He was at her gate one day when he heard her speak.

"Please bring the horse in," she said.

Jack went up to the intercom and listened in astonishment.

"It is a *white* horse, isn't it?" the voice went on. "I specially asked for a white horse."

Jack shuffled on his feet and looked around. Who was she speaking to?

"And fourteen hands? It mustn't be more than that, you know."

Jack puzzled for a minute and then spoke.

"Hello," he said. "I have no horse."

Amy, the girl inside, gasped. "I—I didn't know anyone was there."

"Then why are you talking to me?" asked Jack.

"I was playing," she said. "I'm Amy—who are you?"

"I'm Jack," said Jack.

In that moment Amy realized she could have more fun playing with a real person than with an imaginary one.

"Not *the* Jack?" she went on.

"*The* Jack—yes," came the answer.

"The one who deals in horses?"

"In horses?"

"Yes—you know, Jack the famous horse-dealer."

At this point the boy decided it was best just to agree.

"Yes, that's right—Jack the famous horse-dealer," he said.

"Well, then," continued Amy, "—where is it?"

"Where is what?"

"The horse!"

"Oh—that. Well, it will take a little while. White and fourteen hands, was it?"

"That's right. And no more than three years old."

"I'll see what I can do," said Jack, and that was the end of the conversation.

Escape

Amy lived with her Uncle Fletcher. Now Fletcher was a wealthy man. He made his fortune by knowing the right price for everything. He would have resented Jack taking scraps from his bin, if he had known about it. Fletcher liked hunting and had a black charger called Nightfall but in her own mind Amy called it Nightmare. He had hunting-hounds, and six times a year he went out on Nightmare to chase foxes. Amy hated living there. She was a nuisance to her Uncle. She cost money. He had to drive her to and from school. He had to feed her and clothe her. She was there because her parents were dead.

He did not love her and made her spend every minute of her time doing homework. Therefore Amy wanted a horse. She wanted to escape.

In a green field, covered with buttercups, there were two white horses grazing, drinking from the stream, and frisking in the sun. A dark-haired boy came up with a loop of roop, lassooed the smaller one round the neck, and led it away. It was a friendly horse, delighted to have company. It was a mare, two and a half years, and fourteen hands. The boy was Jack. The horses stayed out all year round. The farmer had planned to train them for work but never got round to it.

Presently the young horse-dealer buzzed on the intercom. He had not expected a man to answer.

"Fletcher," said the man gruffly, as if no other word were needed.

"Jack," replied the boy.

"Who is this?" demanded the owner of the house.

Jack thought for a moment. He had already said his name once and the man did not seem to understand it. He said it again.

"Jack who?" came back the angry reply. "And what do you want?"

"Amy, please."

"Amy?! Who is this? Is this a joke?!"

Jack did not like speaking to adults if he could avoid it. He thought this was the worst adult voice he had ever heard and so he stepped back. The owner of the voice might come out in person soon. Jack's lane was not far away. He went back there and consulted with the horse.

If you had sharp eyes and had been at the side of Amy's house that night, you would have seen a youthful figure climbing up a twisting stem of ivy. Then you would have heard a dog yelp below. For Miter did not want to left behind.

"Shht! Miter! You can't come up!" hissed Jack.

Miter retreated back through the loose railing to where the horse was waiting on the road.

Jack had looked carefully to see which one was Amy's window and when he reached it he saw her sitting at her homework. He tapped lightly. She jumped about ten feet in the air and clapped her hand over her mouth, which was lucky as it prevented her from shouting.

Jack waved his arms and mouthed the words, "It's me, Jack. I've brought your horse."

She might have accidentally pushed him off when she opened the window, but for the fact that he was clinging on with his legs like a koala to a eucalyptus.

"I didn't really mean you to get a horse!" she exclaimed. "I was only playing!"

Jack was puzzled at this. "I'll take it away then," he said.

"No! Don't do that... I didn't mean... I mean—how old is it?"

"Two years."

"How big is it?"

"Fourteen hands."

"What—what colour is it?"

"White. I thought you asked for a white horse."

"I did. I can't believe it!"

"Well, come and see. The horse is down below."

It took some time to persuade Amy to climb down the ivy—she was scared of heights—but when she heard that Jack had spoken to Uncle Fletcher she instantly made up her mind.

"He'll be keeping guard now," she said, "and watching *me* even more closely." She studied Jack's whole appearance. "What will your parents say?"

"I don't have any," said Jack.

"No parents—oh!"

"I live on my own with Miter."

"Who's Miter?"

"My dog."

Through the open window came the sound of a horse whinnying.

"There's the horse," said Jack.

The dog barked.

"That's Miter."

"Oh no," cried Amy. "They'll have to be quiet. If Uncle Fletcher's hounds hear them, they'll be torn to pieces!"

"We'd better hurry, then. Come on—I'll help you."

It was a difficult climb down, with Amy being scared of heights, but when at last they did get to the loose railing, Miter yelped with delight. Almost immediately an angry barking erupted from inside an iron shed.

"Quick!" shouted Amy. "It's Boxer and Punch! If Uncle Fletcher comes out he'll let them loose!"

Jack moved the railing and they scrambled through. A moment later a spotlight came on in the yard behind them and Uncle Fletcher's silhouette appeared in the doorway, magnified by the light.

"Boxer! Punch! Be quiet!" boomed the same voice Jack had so disliked earlier. The dogs quietened down. The figure loomed large and black. Jack and Amy crouched down in the bushes. Jack thought he knew Fletcher from somewhere. It might have been a dream or—a nightmare.

Fletcher patrolled the yard for a minute or two then went back in. "Stop your nonsense now!" he shouted at the dogs from the doorway.

"We should be safe now," whispered Amy. "He won't suspect me. He thinks I'm up in my room doing my homework. Let's go!"

Neighbours

They set off down the road. A yellowish moonlight bathed the horse. Miter made friends with Amy. Jack's feet scuffed the stones on the lane and he shyly asked her about her home. Amy explained how her parents had died and what life was like with Uncle Fletcher.

"Now you can see why I have to run away," she said.

Jack's eyes grew wide. "I can help you," he offered, "if you want me to."

"Of course I do," answered the girl. "Only we mustn't waste time. Let's get on the horse now!"

Jack was not really a rider. When he saw a pony alone in a field he would sometimes steal a ride on its back but he had never actually tried to ride *this* horse. However he was ready for anything, and it *was* such a friendly animal.

"I got the horse for you," he said, "so I'll try first."

He mounted it easily. Miter tilted his head and whimpered at the sight.

"It's good," said Jack.

Almost immediately, the horse hopped on all four feet and Jack tumbled down.

"Are you all right?" asked Amy, helping him up again.

"She's not used to it," observed Jack.

Amy smiled slyly. "And I thought you were Jack the famous horse-dealer!"

"I am, but I don't think the horse has heard about it yet."

"Well look," said Amy, "I think *I'd* better try. You see I have *experience*."

"I'm glad," said Jack, with a twinkle in his eye. "I'll help you up."

If Amy thought her dream had come true when she climbed up on to the horse's back and whispered sweetly in its ear, she was soon woken up. The horse pranced again very primly, and Amy went flying.

Jack picked her up. "I thought you had experience," he said.

"I *do*," replied Amy, "but I don't think the horse has."

The moonlight shone gently where the entrance to Jack's house lay hidden between ferns, long grass, and roses.

"Oh—oh!" sobbed Amy suddenly. "How am I ever going to escape?"

"Never mind," said Jack, "we can go to my house now and then escape tomorrow."

Amy looked around for the first time.

"Is this where you live? I've never been here before."

"Not many people have."

"Don't you get lonely living in a whole big house by yourself?"

"Not me. I've got Miter. And, by the way, you'd better see my house before you say anything else. This is it here."

He pulled back the leafy ferns and branches.

"*This* is where you live?!"

"This is it. Do you want to come in?"

Eyes wide with amazement Amy crawled in behind Jack. She discovered the sheep's wool and lay her head on it. She found the fleece and the moss and the dried grass. It was a long, long time since she had known anything so comfortable. There was enough room for both of them and for Miter, who snuggled up in the middle.

"The horse will be fine," said Jack. "We should go to sleep now."

Amy lay awake for a long time with her eyes open. She could not get used to her new freedom. But at the same time she kept hearing strange rustling and nibbling noises.

"Jack?" she said in a low voice. "What's *that*?"

"Don't worry," answered the boy. "It's just the neighbours. They're a little bit noisy."

"*Neighbours*?!" exclaimed Amy in alarm.

"Yes, rabbits."

"Oh!" There was silence for a minute then, "Jack..?"

"Yes?"

"It's dark."

"I know. Sometimes it's too dark for me too. That's why I built something special at the back. Follow me."

He pulled himself up into the second 'room'. Amy followed. Then he moved aside a wooden 'skylight'. Amy stared directly up into the most blazing heaven she had ever seen.

Chapter Two—Into the Forest

Amy was riding the white horse. Jack walked along beside her. After a while he climbed up too. The horse was now easy to ride. Jack held Mitre in his arms. They rode through the trees.

"Look," said Jack, after a time, "we're there. The heart of the forest..."

Neither of them knew how this had happened or how the horse had changed. But it mattered to them very much that they had arrived here.

Jack tethered the horse to a branch. He trod softly over the thick green grass—green in the moonlight—and spied three disused towers. He went into the first tower. A large oak chest lay on the floor. Amy came to his side. He lifted the lid. In the dim shadows he saw it was filled with old drinking goblets. He picked one up and blew off the dust. A jewel shone in a patch of plain tarnished gold. He rubbed the cup on his sleeve but could not clean off any more of the deeply ingrained dust. He put it back and shut the lid.

Without speaking they went into the second tower. There stood a second wooden chest. Amy opened it. It was full of cutlery: knives and forks. She took one piece in her hands, blew on it and polished. A gleam of silver emerged from the dark stains. But try as she might, no more of the dirt would come off.

In the last stone tower they found a third chest. Together they raised the lid. There were books inside—large old volumes, discoloured with dampness. In one place they could clearly see lines of gold tooled into the leather.

Suddenly Amy leapt back into the shadows.

"A horse!" she cried. "It's UncleFletcher! He's following us!"

They both heard the pounding of hoofs.

"It's Nightmarel!"

They ran out together and re-mounted their own horse.

"Miter!" Jack vaulted down to scoop up the little dog in his arms.

The white horse carried them securely away. Jack glimpsed a black horse galloping through the woods, but presently the sound vanished. At length they returned home and soon were curled up safely inside Jack's house.

Daybreak

Amy woke up beneath the open skylight.

The first thing she said was, "The horse!"

"The horse?" said Jack sleepily. Miter licked his face. "What about it?"

"We rode it!"

"Did we?"

"Don't you remember? We went into the heart of the forest."

"Oh—yes."

"Has there always been a forest there?"

"I don't know."

"You've lived here all your life and you've never seen a forest?"

"Well..."

They pulled themselves out through the opening of Jack's house. The white horse was grazing sweetly nearby. The green grass glistened with dew in the sunlight.

"*Daybreak*!" whispered Amy. "I think that's what we should call her."

"It's a nice name," said Jack. "I agree."

"But Jack," she went on. "If I don't go home now, Uncle Fletcher will notice I've been missing."

Jack realized he did not want her to go away.

"You have to escape," he said.

"Yes, but not until tonight."

Jack remembered his glimpse of black horse.

"Who *was* that—?" he started to say.

"—It *might* have been my uncle," answered Amy. "But if it was he won't remember. Not yet."

Jack agreed without knowing why.

The Old Man

The shadows grew longer and longer and still Amy did not

come. At last Jack flopped down on the grass.

The moon was higher in the sky when Daybreak nudged him. He knew it was time to go, even without Amy. Jack rose, leaving his flattened shape in the grass. Daybreak carried him straight into the heart of the forest...

The moon shone again on the three towers but this time Jack did not get down to look. The horse did not want him to, he thought. Nothing moved. Suddenly, he saw a shadow. It flitted out from between the trees. Soon, the shape became an old man, with long beard and grey robe. He crossed the clearing between the towers. The dark grass hardly breathed beneath his feet. He raised his hand to touch the horse. She lowered her brow to meet his fingers.

Jack felt the warm night air hugging his form. He was not uncomfortable with the stranger. He listened hard for what the old man would say. But when the man did look up, Jack felt very unsettled. His face was like a white cliff lit by the moon. The eyes peered deeply into him.

Jack seemed to know even before the old man spoke, what it was he was going to say.

"Build me a shelter," said the old man, "build it simple and build it strong. Make its walls thin, and its roof light. Do this for me."

The horse turned. She had listened too, with horse's ears, and knew what to do. Before hardly any time had passed she returned Jack to his space in the grass.

A Shelter

The idea of the shelter rose in him again the next day. He felt its springiness. He saw through its walls. He reached down with its roots. It would be a *woven* house, colourful and fresh, with leafy windows and rafters light as air. He would make it out of willow.

"That's it, Miter!" he cried, and the dog cocked his head to listen. "A willow house! We'll make a *living* shelter for the old man!"

"Woof!" Miter did not understand but he knew a good idea when he heard one.

"We'll plant the willows in the shape of a hut and tie them at the top. It'll have air for the walls and leaves to cover it when it starts growing!"

"Woof!" repeated Miter.

Amy Returns

Amy had been absent for a good reason. Her picture of Daybreak, Jack and Miter slipped away. Her Uncle kept coming up the stairs and putting his ear to her door. The ivy looked thin, the window very high above the ground. She sang by herself, looking out of the window. Then she saw the moon rise.

Amy felt stronger the following night. She chose to climb down the ivy. She had decided to find Jack again.

When she saw the willow shelter her eyes grew wide and round.

"It's what he wanted," said Jack and he told Amy the whole story.

"Will you plant it there?" she asked.

"Yes. And twine the stems around to make it stand."

"Will its roots grow?"

"When it rains. And then the leaves will come out."

"How do you know?"

"I've seen people doing it. I've seen lots of things."

Amy helped but soon Jack was yawning.

"Have a rest before we go," she said, and Jack went to lie down in his house. When Amy crawled in to fetch him all she could hear was his soft breathing from the straw.

The Willow House

The bundle of willow was tied and ready. The horse stood waiting. Daybreak carried Amy to the heart of the forest, where Jack had been the night before... She chose her spot carefully. Then she planted the willow. Stem by stem she dug it into the ground. She wove it together, in the way Jack had shown her. She created a little door. The windows formed themselves. The 'walls' curled up over the top. They were made out of panels of air. She tied them off at the top.

Amy worked for a long time. When she heard the pounding of hoofs again, she was reluctant to move. She had made a dwelling. It was a good place to stay. Only it was not her place. It was meant for the old man. Daybreak took her back.

"His shelter's ready?" cried Jack in astonishment.

"Yes, I finished it just in time. The black horse came again."

"Did it look right—the shelter?"

"Oh Jack! It was just perfect!"

"Did you see the old man?"

"I didn't. But I think he was there somewhere. I wish he could help us—why do we always have to get chased away?"

"We have to find out more about the things in the three towers. The old man has something to do with them. And so does the black rider."

"Jack, I have to go back home again. It's still early and Uncle Fletcher won't be up yet."

"But Amy—I'm ready to go on. I don't really want to live in my old house any more."

"I know. But we can only escape—I mean go into the forest—if we have our own home to travel in. And then we have to escape from—the Black Rider, you called him."

"Well, I'll do anything you say," said Jack. And Amy left.

The Caravan

Jack put his mind to it. She had said 'our own home to travel in'. He put his boots on and thought. He walked in the open air. He walked and he thought. And then he knew.

It stood there like a dusty jewel. A seat for two (and a dog) at the front, a half-door at the back. A table inside, and a little stove with a chimney. It was a gypsy caravan. It belonged to the old Folk Park.

The gypsy caravan rested there in a shed with no light. Jack had seen it many times.

His brown eyes danced. He touched it, then hopped away, scuffling the straw and dust with his feet. Miter barked at him.

"Quiet now, dog, someone will come!"

He rubbed its lamp with his sleeve. He spat on it and rubbed again until the brass shone. Then he opened the shed doors at the back. Shafts of evening sunlight poured in. Daybreak the horse stopped her grazing and looked up.

"I don't believe it!" exclaimed Amy. "I just don't believe it!"

"It's been sitting there for ages," said Jack. "No one cared about it."

Amy pushed open the half-door with a finger. She went inside and opened the lid of the stove.

"Ashes."

A tear rolled down her cheek.

"I'm so happy, Jack!" she said.

The old iron kettle was the last thing they scrubbed. Some flakes of rust fell out. The moon was high in the sky now. They hung the kettle on the hook at the back and were ready.

Just before leaving Amy tried the mattress.

"It's horsehair," said Jack. He knelt on the floor beside her and lay his head on the pillow.

In the Forest

The caravan rolled on, cracking twigs and flattening tracks on the forest floor. Nobody drove.

They crossed a root, and Amy bumped awake.

"We're there!" she said.

"What? Where?" woke Jack.

"Here. In the forest..."

Miter shuffled sleepily to his feet. The horse had stopped.

"I dreamt about it," went on Amy. "Daybreak was there, looking into the willow shelter. The old man came out. He went to the three towers. The place was very busy suddenly. People were coming from all directions. The old man pointed them in. They poured into the chests and disappeared. And then I thought I heard the horse speak. 'How old am I?' she said. 'Two years only,' I replied but a voice behind me said, 'Older than you can possibly imagine'. It seemed so real, I looked for whoever it was who spoke but no one was there. It feels as if they are still there."

Jack believed her. He went out into the clearing to look. But nobody was there. He smelt the willow growing. The shelter was strong. Would the old man not come back? Jack listened. Miter listened. How many people can fit into a chest? Jack wondered.

"Here you are," he said, feeding Miter a handful of bread

19

from his pocket. "We're all hungry."

Jack spotted a silver horn in the trees. Something whispered. Looking up he saw, full in the face, a living unicorn.

It was human, or intelligent. Not a horse.

Jack stared and stared. Then he saw only moonlight.

He whistled to Miter.

"Come on, boy."

Amy had collected the kettle and filled it with water.

"We'll have tea," she said.

Jack built a fire. Amy toasted bread. The colour of the tea was a mild clover. Hearing things around him, Jack wished for a way of answering new creatures.

"More tea?" said Amy.

There was such a whirling and stirring next they did not know what to do. It was as if black flurries of snow were falling then a minute later white. The Black Rider loomed large over Amy and the unicorn appeared beside Jack.

"Uncle Fletcher!" cried Amy.

"No!" said Jack.

He stared into the eyes of the unicorn again and saw hundreds of things which he could not name. Hoofbeats pounded away behind him. Amy had gone. He could not take his eyes off the snowy white flock which was the unicorn's skin.

Chapter Three—The Unicorn-Boy

Daybreak was pleased to see the old man coming out of his willow shelter. They talked together for a minute, in their own way, the horse with nudges, the man with words, and then the old man turned to watch Jack. He looked so small there, the boy in the power of the unicorn.

Jack clung to the side of the caravan. The unicorn's dark eye studied him. Then the creature turned and walked to the entrance of the caravan. The door was open. The unicorn climbed in. The timbers creaked, the caravan rocked, then, mysteriously, it grew still.

Miter crept up to his master's side and whimpered.

"What is it, boy?" said Jack, in a daze.

"Amy's gone," is what the dog wanted to say.

Miter went into the caravan. Jack followed as far as the steps. There was no sign of the unicorn. A boy was lying on the bed. Miter went up to him and licked his hand. The boy lifted his brown eyes and smiled briefly at Jack and his dog.

Over at the other side of the clearing, the old hermit held the reins. He stood with Daybreak watching the caravan. Jack came over to speak to him.

"Miter knows that boy," said Jack.

"Yes," said the old man. "But watch."

A moment later the dog came out followed by the uni-corn-boy.

Jack saw it this way: first there was the boy, then there was moonlight, then there was a unicorn. Seconds later the uni-corn had disappeared, back into the woods.

"*In the heart of the forest you are here to stay*," said the old man. "What will you do?"

Jack knelt down beside Miter.

"What shall we do, boy?" he said.

The dog turned towards where the unicorn had gone, and barked.

"He wants to follow it," said Jack.

"Then I give you my good wishes."

"Miter will follow the scent."

"Go quickly then, for the scent will soon be gone. Find what the boy can tell you."

Jack fled into the forest but he never once caught sight of the unicorn.

A Coracle

The scent led them down to the shore of a lake. A coracle—a little boat for one—lay beached there on the sand. Jack spotted the unicorn at last, moving swiftly round the shore.

"The trees are too thick," he said. He looked at the boat. "It belongs to the old man—I know it does. We'll use it to go over the lake."

22

He pushed the coracle into the water and climbed in. Miter jumped in beside him, rocking the boat—Jack struggled to keep his balance, but soon the water settled into gentle ripples underneath them. With his paddle dipping on either side Jack floated out into the moonlight.

Half way across he thought he heard voices rising from the bottom of the lake, but he could not make out what they were saying. Jack was a boy who believed everything that happened to him. He had never been told not to. It was still the first night of Jack and Amy's escape into the forest.

He looked up at the tall trees on the mountainside.

"Timber," he thought out loud. "Enough timber for a castle."

The whole mountain looked like a great black crown.

Then he looked up at the sky.

"The stars need stories," he said, "or we will never come to the end."

Miter probably agreed but he did not say so.

Each dip of the oar let new whispers rise up from the lake. Jack told stories as they went.

"Just around that point," he said at last. "We should see more then." And when they reached it they saw a castle standing in a ring of mountains.

There was a shimmer of green, followed by a loop of purple, which then turned white—it was the unicorn going among the shadows, tracing its path along the shore. Jack's heart beat faster. His little boat slapped against the waves he made with rowing. Then suddenly Miter jumped—splash!—

and swam to the stones. Jack dragged the coracle ashore and, without hesitation, climbed up to the castle.

Dream-Doors

He stopped at the entrance, trying to make up his mind.

"You see, Miter, these are dream-doors," he said. "When the unicorn went through them he might have changed into something else. If I go in I might change too. And what would happen to you?"

However, the dog was not disturbed by the idea. He pushed with his nose against the door and it inched open. Both dog and boy went in.

The floor was made of green stone. Miter's claws tapped on it. But the sound of the lake also blew through the hall. Waves lapped, and hushed again. Beams of moonlight shone in. Through the glassless windows, boughs of trees and bushes shivered into the castle itself.

"What kind of person lives here?" wondered Jack.

Suddenly a voice sang out.

"Amy!" cried Jack, running to the stairway. Halfway up the stairs a vast window opened out over the lake. But Jack did not stop to admire the view. He flew on to the top. The first thing he saw was the coracle and the old man, then in an alcove he saw Daybreak. Jack cleared his dizzy head and knew what he was seeing were just ripples reflecting from the lake. He breathed hard and shut his eyes. When he opened them again a boy with dark curly hair and brown eyes was standing before him. It was the unicorn-boy. Once more Miter went up to him and licked his hand.

Gusts of wind blew through the upper landing.

"I heard you calling out," said the boy. "There is no Amy here—only Jack."

Jack listened in astonishment. The other boy did indeed have Jack's own shape, his own face and his own hair. Miter loved him too—and that was proof.

The unicorn-boy went on.

"This castle is my home. When I am in it I am a boy like you. Exactly like you. But when I go out I am a unicorn."

"And what about the caravan?" questioned Jack.

"In the caravan or in any kind of house you choose to make, I become a boy again."

Jack felt new courage and thought of Amy.

"Is it true that I will find my friend again?" he asked.

The unicorn-boy knelt down and stroked Miter.

"Wherever she is," he said, "you will find her."

"The Black Rider took her away."

"I know. I was there too. I saw it"

"*Why* were you there?" Jack was thinking about the unicorn's dark eye gazing at him.

"I was there because of the willow house. I came to see it and then I found the caravan."

"Are you really Jack? How can you be?"

"Come here and listen. I will tell you my story from the beginning."

He led Jack into the alcove on the upstairs landing of the

25

castle. They sat down together and the unicorn-boy began his story.

A Story

"Look around you," he said. Jack looked into the darkness of the landing. "There was once a great dark space," went on the boy, "and behind the space there were names and names and names, waiting. 'Come here,' said a voice, and the names all came. 'I have something to tell you'."

Jack imagined the names as if they were coming out from behind the dark pillars on the landing of the castle. The boy continued.

"The voice became a white horse and a rider. The horse began to walk. Wherever it walked crystals appeared. Some names came to the crystals. Others became their colours, blue, red and green. The horse began to trot, and spears of grass appeared around the crystals. Some of the names ran to the grass and others became the scent of flowers, rose and lilac and jasmine. When the horse began to canter, little snouts appeared between the stones. Some names flew to whiskers, some to fur, and some to little beady eyes. At last the rider galloped and the first true men and women appeared. The names came to their holy tasks. The White Rider saw what he had done and was glad.

"But then the rider dressed in black, on a black horse, jumped down with a crash from the sound-filled space, and spoke *his* name. Then every name forgot the voice that had called it and heard only this one.

"Times have gone by and everything has its coat of names. The Black Rider gallops too. And nothing seems to be the way it was. The White Rider came in one clear flash—but now is gone.

"Lastly, like a twinkle in his eye, he thought of me. And many names came close to be *my* thoughts.

" 'You are the Hearer by the Lake,' said the White Rider, 'and you must listen to the creatures I have made—to every sound they make.'

"I listened well, and all the names of things rose up from the lake to my ears. But one day as I set foot in the water the Black Rider dipped his horse's hoofs into the same stream. The soft air I had heard the voices in, grew black. I felt that I would never whisper to their names again. Then there were four legs standing in the stream, and I saw that they were mine—I had a coat of hair, a mane, and dew-filled eyes. I had become a horse and would have stayed forever black if nothing else had happened. But higher up, where light is born and mountains watch over it, the White Rider reached down his arm and stroked the water. My skin turned white, a horn grew on my head and the dew fell from my eyes. I was a unicorn.

"Now every time I find a home built by human hands I become a boy again. I loved your willow shelter most of all."

"Amy built it," interrupted Jack.

"I know. It was too small for me to go in. But the caravan seemed right."

The trees curled up in their roots outside. Jack felt a film of blackness coming over his eyes. Perhaps he would have hugged the boy but everything grew faint and disappeared.

The White Rider

Miter licked the sleep from Jack's eyes. At first Jack thought it was the unicorn. He was lying close to the shore. The castle and the boy had vanished. He went down to the lake and stood in the water. His feet remained the same, his legs were his own, nothing about him changed. Miter ran into the lake and splashed delightedly. It was daylight now.

Jack and Miter ate the last pieces of bread and chocolate in his knapsack. There was plenty of water to drink. They played at skimming stones. Jack threw them and Miter jumped after them. Jack still had no one to look after him.

"Now we know who stole away Amy," he said after a minute. "The Black Rider."

Later on, far out in the water again, the little boat stooped to one side and the lake began to pour in. Whoops! In one swift second the water jumped in and Jack and Miter fell out. The poor boy was lost. The last things he saw were the gold and silver threads of the ripples above him.

It was the White Rider who saved him. Jack gulped in hungry mouthfuls of air. An old story told again, the best of stories—it was like that for Jack when he saw the White Rider's face.

Jack dizzily shook the drops of water from his eyes. He was in the arms of the White Rider, on the back of the White Rider's horse. It was like being in a palace. They were going up the side of a glass mountain, Jack thought.

"Why does the horse not slip?" he wondered.

"Courage," said the White Rider.

"The horse *is* courage," thought Jack, "that's what he means." Jack was not surprised that the White Rider knew what he was thinking.

They went into a cave of paintings. The paintings on the wall showed the story the unicorn-boy had told. They showed other true things too.

"We are in the Cave of Hours," said the White Rider, and Jack knew that this meant every minute of time was on the walls. If you looked at them slowly they seemed to come alive.

Jack stopped abruptly at a picture of himself with Miter, at his old house.

"That's me!" he cried. "And Miter... and," he looked a little further on, "and Amy." His voice tailed off. "Where is Amy?" he asked softly.

"Come further into the cave," said the White Rider.

Jack followed. He came to the chest of books, the chest of cups, and the chest of cutlery.

"I don't understand," he said.

"Amy is in there," answered the White Rider.

Jack opened the first chest. Such a light came from it, he felt faint. He opened the second one, and felt fainter still. He opened the third chest, and fainted away altogether.

Miter the dog smiled—if a dog can smile—into the face of the White Rider. They sat at the entrance to the Cave of Hours.

"You came early to this cave," said the White Rider. "Your picture is one of the first there. Where would people be without you?"

Neither of them spoke then—for dogs can speak at times—but Miter sidled right up under the White Rider's arm.

At length, perhaps minutes or even hours later, the White Rider broke the silence.

"You will take him there, Miter, won't you? You know the way."

Chapter Four—The Castle

"Miter-r-r!!" called Jack, but the dog would not listen. He was now so far ahead Jack gave up trying to see him. But then the little dog would stop and sit where Jack could spy him, before leaping up and taking off again. Jack plunged on, in breathless chase, for now the dog was master of the 'man'.

Many minutes later Miter stopped and Jack flopped down beside him.

"What did you do that for?" the boy asked, but no sooner had he said it than he looked up and saw the wall of a great castle. It was green in the sun, with moss and lichen and—ivy.

Immediately Jack knew Amy was inside.

Miter seemed content at having done his job and lay in the warm sunshine. Jack climbed.

He reached the window high up the side of the wall and pulled himself in. He was not in Amy's room but he was near her.

He stood in a passage of doors, each one with a key in its lock. Jack had never known doors, in his short life, only 'ways in'. Amy herself was a way in for Jack. It had not occurred to him that people could close like doors. He was going to try each door in turn but something stopped him. He felt afraid.

He thought Miter was dead. The fear was like a cold hand on the pit of his stomach. The dark dread had something to do with the stairs.

Jack believed he was the poorest boy in the world at that moment. And then he saw the truth: something coming up the stairs was poorer than him. It really had no heart.

He was the White Rider's brother. Jack struggled to understand. The Black Rider was not dressed in black. He wore green, mauve, and blue. His jewels—around his hands and belt and neck—flashed with colours from distant places. Where was the black? Jack thought this handsome man might be his father.

The Black Rider opened the door of one of the rooms and went in. Jack himself slipped down the little stairway he found behind him.

Mertha the Shiner

The stairs led down a shaft, like a well, to a little door at the foot. It was a forgotten door, Jack thought. A single gleam of gold shone through the narrow opening. Jack peeped in.

A very old man sat there, in impossible gloom. His eyes were screwed up. He held a cup of gold in his hands. A tiny light stood beside him.

The old man sat up with a start. He fixed a pair of spectacles on his nose.

"This is not what I expected," he said.

Jack gazed. "What did you not expect?" he asked.

"A visit from a boy your age."

Jack suddenly did not know why he was there.

The old man peered at him. "Just when I thought I was going to die," he said.

Jack's eyes grew accustomed to the light. There were plates and cups of gold stacked around the room. A dirty tapestry hung on the wall, with a picture of a unicorn on it.

"I am Mertha," said the old man, "the Shiner."

Jack thought for a minute. "What age *am* I?" he asked.

Mertha stayed silent but Jack remembered a voice saying, "Older than you can possibly imagine."

"I am very old," said Mertha, as if he had heard a different question. "Where is your home?"

"My home," answered Jack, "is a box in the ground that opens into a burrow. I live there with Miter. But then I left my home and went in a caravan with Amy. Amy has been stolen by—her uncle, and I am trying to get her back."

"Don't you know anyone older than yourself?"

"No," said Jack.

"Then we are the same. I knew it when you came in."

"What does it mean to be a Shiner?" asked Jack.

"A Shiner gives up all his life to the colour of gold."

"Have *you* given up all you life?"

"I have."

Jack thought to himself, "Miter would be a good Shiner

with his coat." Then he said out loud, "What do you do when you go out?"

"Well, I never do," replied Mertha. "I am here till I die."

"As long as that! Have you never been anything else except a Shiner?"

"Oh, I have been a boy like you once. I lived near here. I walked in the green glades. I knew this castle. The man who owns it wanted me to work for him. To start with I was free to go out if I wanted to. But then, when I did his work for him I began to see the gleam of gold. Just a glimmer under the layer of grime. And after that I could not stop. I tried everything I knew to make the gleam shine through. Heaven knows where he gets them from, all these plates and cups."

Jack remembered Amy's dream and the people diving into the chest.

"My master understood me well," went on Mertha. "He knew I would go on working all my life. All my shining leads to one result—the gold gleams brightly underneath the gloom, as if far away in the distance."

"My friend is *here*," said Jack suddenly.

"Yes. My master needs her."

"The Black Rider is your master."

"He is."

"He needs her to polish the gold, doesn't he? To do the bit that you can't do—to make it shine through to the surface."

"Yes. The job that I have tried to do all my life. He needs her youth, her goodness. He will wipe the gold with them."

"Amy!" cried Jack.

"Don't start up so suddenly!" snapped Mertha. "The Amy you knew is not there any more. He is working on her, changing her, and then he will use what he has taken to put the final sparkle on the gold!"

"I have to save her!"

"Why? She has everything she needs. And you—stay here and help *me* with my work!"

Jack recoiled in disgust. "Stay here? Grow old and die like you?"

"You might as well. The gold is calling out for you as well."

"No!" said Jack. "Never!" And he went back out through the door, leaving Mertha chuckling to himself.

Not Altogether There

Amy had wished for nothing else but to make tea for Jack, with Daybreak grazing behind her, and the freshly-painted colours of the caravan dancing in the firelight.

A black storm swept her up. She thought, 'Uncle Fletcher!' and imagined her old imprisonment starting again. Then she saw the truth. Her captor was vast and empty, far greater than her uncle's house.

Amy's dreams were dashed. A tear came into her eye.

Jack went back up to rescue Amy. She mattered to him more than gold. The stairs and doors could not keep him away from her.

But Amy was not altogether there.

He saw her standing far, far away like the distant shine of metal Mertha could never quite attain.

Jack stretched out his hand.

The castle shook with footsteps. Voices pressed in from the walls.

"Shine my gold!" they hissed.

Jack looked into Amy's eyes and saw her disappear completely.

One voice sang out beyond the others. Amy recognised that sound. She stepped towards an opening at the wall. She might have had silk slippers on her feet, her steps were so light.

On the stairway itself the voice divided and became a choir.

Before the morning star had left the sky, before the glimmering sun laid dewdrops on the grass, this lost girl found her home.

Tears

Miter had slept at the foot of the ivy. He heard a voice singing. It was a woman's voice. At the same moment he saw the castle wall open and Amy step out. The woman called her. Amy ran to meet her and they embraced.

Miter shrugged off the sleep. Amy and the woman went lightly among the flowers. Miter heard their voices by the trees. They walked so deeply in the garden no power on earth could touch them.

Amy vanished through the door again. Miter curled up in his dream and fell asleep.

Jack saw that Amy would not be the Black Rider's servant. He felt sure Amy would be safe. He wanted her to be his friend again but could not break through the magic of the castle.

Jack climbed down the ivy. He wept tears of joy and tears of sorrow into Miter's coat.

Chapter Five—A Watermill

The dark pages start with Jack's exit from the castle. But written on those pages, in golden letters, certain words shine out. TRUTH and JUSTICE are two of those. For Jack had no one left to follow.

He saw a deep river. It came over the hill and down. Its water was rich and peaty, the colour of wine. Jack could not help it—he wanted to throw himself in.

The river flowed on. Now rising, now falling, now rippled, now flat, but always deep. On its way it slowed to taste the cool, sweet soil on either bank.

Miter drank.

The river coursed on, doubling itself with every bend. It arched its back to see the dry fields. It pushed, with its weed-ed feet, to race around the hill.

It listened with its fluent ears pinned back, to a call from times long past. "Do not forget me," pressed the voice, "although you pour your heart into the deep blue sea, do not forget me." And as it flowed the river remembered, how as a tiny spring, it had bubbled up newborn beneath the feet of the White Rider's horse.

The river reached a great dark stone. It surged around it,

curled its fingers over every bump, pushed upon it and judged its weight.

"Now," thought the river, "the sun adores me, the fish count their blessings, the trees drink from my banks. But this stone has no hope."

And, with a heart full of strength, the river rolled the stone down into the black water's foot. It tumbled blindly then rolled on inch by inch.

Now at the edge of a mossy brink, the great stone leapt. Down it plunged again through green to blue then black, and prised itself beneath a wooden heel.

The Millwheel

Nothing could lift Jack's spirits or waken him from his gloom. Miter jumped repeatedly then fell into silence.

Then suddenly below them they saw a vast millwheel which once had turned but now was still. No bread, no flour, no corn—the huge quern stones inside the mill stood silent. Though its roofs gleamed with sunshine the quiet of the tomb filled the old watermill. Somewhere on the chaff floor a mouse squeaked. The cat, sleeping at the loft doors, raised an eyebrow. No one stirred.

Jack could not feel any interest in it.

All at once a white horse galloped down and drank from the millpond.

"Daybreak!" cried Jack. "Is it really you?"

He examined the horse's markings and gazed into its eyes.

"It is you!"

"Is this your horse?" asked a voice out of nowhere.

Jack looked up. A woman stood beside him. She wore a pointed hat, had cold green eyes and was slightly out of breath.

"Because if it is you have a bill to pay."

Jack hardly knew what to say. "It's Amy's horse," he replied.

"Then would you please tell Amy to settle her account?" went on the woman. "Every night this horse comes here and eats our grass. There is no common grazing round the mill. Everyone knows that. And if they don't we tell them. I've chased this horse so many times now!"

The woman eyed Jack closely. His black curly hair and open face stood out against Daybreak's snowy flank.

"Where is Amy?" she asked.

Jack had his mouth open ready to reply but then stopped. Amy was in the soft sounds of the river he had ignored, she was in the rapid water, in the cooling air. Amy was here.

"Have you lost your tongue?" said the woman sharply.

"She'll be coming soon," said Jack.

"Are you weak?" she went on. "Can you work?"

"I've built a house and trained a horse."

"And what's your name?"

"Jack. I'm very hungry."

"Well, Jack-I'm-very-hungry, I am Joan. I run this mill alone. No one argues with me or my decision. Put your horse in through that gate and come inside."

Jack followed. Joan fed him a strange sauce of wheat berries then took him to the winnowing loft. Jack had never seen the insides of a watermill before.

"The silence is deafening," muttered Joan. "The wheel doesn't turn, the stones won't grind. What use is a mill without movement? So—take this broom. We'll do our spring-cleaning. Not a speck of dust is to remain!"

Dreams

Jack swept the floor. He picked out the grains of corn from between the floorboards. There was a barking from below. Miter knew where Jack was. Jack looked out the loft door. There was Miter looking up. Daybreak was frisking in the narrow paddock by the river.

"I'll be there soon," called Jack, then his attention was caught by the millwheel. A flood of water was pouring down and through it. The wheel was continually creaking but would not move.

"What is wrong with it?" wondered Jack. But then almost immediately he heard a sobbing welling up from the mill below.

"Who's that?" Jack asked himself. Only Joan the miller was in the house.

Now Jack woke into a dream. The dark corners of the attic burst with distant music. He felt a movement of hands or wings around his head. The sobbing stopped as if it had been his own. A voice said, "Deeper down the water flows," and Jack saw himself in a swirling current pushing against a blackness.

Then he fell into a real sleep and dreamt the unicorn came through the wall. Its head changed into the boy who looked like himself but the body stayed as a horse. "Let's go," said the boy, "or your life will lose you!"

Jack snapped awake. "How can my life lose me?" he wondered. But it was dark outside and he had slept for hours.

Starshine and river-music appeared through the loft door equally softly.

Jack stared down. The moon left green sickles on the back of the millwheel, where rainwater had collected.

A man appeared, a figure from the grass. Jack looked for the earthy cavern he might have sprung from. He was tall and thin, stooping like the moonlight. He wore a round hat and an apron with pockets. Jack watched, fascinated, as the man leaned his long length against the millwheel and pushed. Then he turned and pushed down on the buckets with his hands. He stopped to wipe his brow. The millwheel would not move. Then from the shadows three more figures appeared. They crept up to the man. Two of them grabbed him by the arms while the third thrust something into his back. The man crumpled and fell to the ground. Jack knew he was dead. The three men filled the apron with stones, threw the body into the deep water at the foot of the millwheel, and ran off.

A murder had been committed. Jack gaped, with big eyes blinking. It was as if he had imagined it, the scene was so still again. They had made no sound, they had risen from the earth. What had he seen?

The smell of antique wood, the sound of water draining from river into millpond, made Jack drowsy again. When next he opened his eyes the sun was shining through morning mist. Jack beat his head with his hands. He missed his dog and did not know where dream began or sleep ended.

A Dive

Joan returned. She knelt and studied the cracks between the floorboards. When she discovered no grains she turned her eye on Jack. He stared back.

"Why do you look at me like that?" she snapped.

Jack thought for a minute. "There's something in the millpond," he said.

Joan started. "What do you mean? What 'something'? What are you talking about?"

Jack grew more and more certain of what he had seen. "Bones and blood," he went on. This was how he imagined the body in the pond.

Joan turned deathly pale. "Are you mad?" she gasped.

"I saw—"

"—Yes, yes, what did you see?"

"—I saw..." Jack was suddenly struck by a thought. "Why does the millwheel not turn?" he asked.

"Am I talking to a born fool?" exploded Joan. "Tell me what you saw?"

"I saw a man who pushed the millwheel to make it turn. But it wouldn't. Then three men killed him and threw him in the pond."

Joan shrieked and clutched at her hair.

"You're lying!" she screamed. "You saw no such thing!"

Jack would not be frightened. He thought only of the body in the pond and something dark lying beside the bones.

"I can get it out for you," he said calmly.

Joan broke down in sobs. Jack realised this was the sound he had heard the night before. Suddenly she broke off.

"Go then!" she shouted. "See what you can get out. It will do you no good and me neither!"

Miter stared very quizzically at Jack as he took off his shoes and his shirt. Joan looked on, eyes narrowed to slits. The sunlight slanted directly at the base of the millwheel.

Jack was a good swimmer from the many summer days splashing with Miter in the water hole near his house. Miter was excited again now, but Jack contemplated the blue eyes of Amy as if she was there with him.

Jack dived in. The cold shock of water on his skin woke him sharply. He swam to the foot till his ears thrummed. The lowest point of the millwheel lay further off still. A blue apron protruded from the mud. Jack pulled it free. The water had dissolved its knots. The stones tumbled from its pockets. Beneath the apron nothing else remained. If there had been flesh it was gone, if there were bones they were buried. No other clothes were visible. Jack swam quickly up.

Black Murder

Joan closed her eyes.

"Why have you come here," she asked, "with your white horse, your dog, and your 'Amy'?"

"There is something blocking the millwheel," was all Jack said.

"Black murder!" cried Joan.

"Let me free it."

"I can't bear it," went on the woman. "My husband John lies dead in the mud. You have his apron in your hands. Every night he comes back to the wheel and puts his shoulder to it. Every night my brothers three return and kill him coldly."

Jack thought about the mill, strangely spotless and still. Its over-deep millpond and nearly-submerged wheel. The apron coming to light.

"Your husband's dead," said Jack, "and a great black rock is stopping the millwheel from turning. Let me spike it." Jack had seen farmers shifting rocks with spikes.

Joan lifted her face from her tear-stained hands.

"And have another death on my conscience? You're too young. If the millwheel turns you'll be dragged into the mud."

"Your husband John is wanting out," said Jack on an impulse.

Joan stared. "I have a metal spike," she said.

There was no stepping-off point into the water, with gradual descent. From the grassy verge the drop was steep and direct to the bed of the pond. Water cascaded in from the channel of the river above, filling the pond with air and sinuous currents.

Jack did not dare throw in the long iron spike for fear of losing it in the mud. He would have to carry it in his hands. He jumped, and its weight dragged him down. He spun round, nearly lost the spike, then found his feet.

His arms grew strong, he felt he was a different soul, a man and not a boy. And in the blackness, lit by gleaming shafts of sun, he saw the dark stone wedged between two shelves or buckets of the wheel. The iron spike jabbed forth from his hands. How could he hope to shatter or dislodge it?

With the lever of the spike he tried to shame the great stone into movement. He stepped into the very centre of the wheel. He prodded, jabbed and pushed. The stone jumped once, the wheel juddered minutely then fell still again. He risked his life.

With whose determination did he stay? Whose breath filled his lungs? Whose strength filled his arms? The stone had moved enough. He crept out from the wheel and swam to face it from the front. He lifted up the spike and with the greatest force that he could muster thrust it at the rock. The dark black shape cracked into pieces, every line of weakness fractured. A vast deep shuddering moved the wheel, the ancient settled mud, the bones of John the miller himself. Jack tumbled, lost the spike, saw the sun burst in a thousand bubbles of churning water. Then he saw no more.

Chapter Six—The Weighing House

The Jack who jumped into the pond was several times younger than the one who came out. He had trouble buttoning up his shirt. Then he saw it was not his own—it was rough, made of horsehair. It was a dark moonless night.

Jack took some steps along the path that led into the forest close by. He walked without thinking, well into the forest.

Shortly he realized that someone had fallen in beside him and was matching his steps. Soon a second man paced along beside him and Jack hardly knew where he came from. Presently a third crept up behind.

"Who are you?" asked Jack.

"Relatives," answered the man to his left.

"I wonder if I've seen you before?"

The man at the back pressed closer. "The river has a long memory," he said. "What it may reveal is nobody's business."

Jack marched like a soldier in a platoon.

"Where are we going?" he enquired.

"Back to beginnings," said the man on his right.

"Yes," said the one behind, "what have you seen?"

"What do you know?" chimed in the voice on the left.

"How much have you learned?" asked the one on the right.

Jack's mind was like an empty grain store.

"I don't understand," he said.

The way into the forest grew darker.

"The weighing-house lies ahead," said the man at the back.

Scales

The slow door opened. Jack glimpsed a lamplight and the backs of several people inside. The last few steps were long as if he were weighed down.

The air inside was thick with talk.

"What are they so noisy about?" asked Jack.

"They want the wheat," answered the first man.

"The wheat germ," added the second.

"For its quality," put in the third.

A set of weighing-scales greeted Jack's eyes. The coppery bucket on the right gleamed as it moved. The dark weights on the other side seemed shadowy and leaden. A huge man stood at the centre, shuffling the weights as if they were pennies.

A great cheer went up when the man poured the grain into the coppery bucket and the scales sank down. The same people who had cheered began to groan when his swift hands shifted more and more weights onto the other side.

Each one came forward with his or her individual pouch.

The huge man filled their bags from the coppery bucket. Jack saw the tears in their eyes or puzzled looks on their faces as the people turned.

"Have they paid for more?" he asked his companions.

"That is what they get," replied the first.

"Not one grain more," confirmed the second.

"Not one grain less," said the third.

The huge man dusted out the coppery bucket then set it down. He picked up a second one, identical to the first, and laid it on the scales.

"That one is for buying," explained the first man.

Now men and women came up with their bags of grain to sell. Time and again the bucket rose quickly on the scales. The huge man took their grain and paid them.

"So little, so little," said one, and others shook their heads, perplexed.

Jack was not sure what the people wanted. The man at his side seemed to read his thoughts.

"They want the value of the corn," he said.

"Will they not get it?"

"He—Joachim—gives them what it is in his power to give."

Jack looked at the three men beside him. Whose 'relatives' were they? They were relatives of each other perhaps. Three brothers.

With elbows and nudges the three men edged Jack towards Joachim.

"I run a tidy house," commented the big man, "and you

are untidy in it. What do you want?"

Jack's feet would not move one way or the other. He looked up at the muscle-bound man.

"I would like to learn to lift weights like you," he replied.

"Look into this bucket," said Joachim. He held up the second of the two buckets. "What do you see?"

Jack looked. He saw the looks of the people who had gone away disappointed.

"Now look into this one," went on the weighing master, holding out the first coppery bucket.

Jack looked in. He did not see the beaten copper. He saw—what was it?—the face of an old man with a polishing cloth. He saw a girl with curls in her hair.

"What do you see?" asked Joachim again.

"I—I don't know," stuttered Jack.

"How much you do not know!" exclaimed the big man.

"Give him a chance," said the first man.

"He will learn," said the second.

"He is willing," added the third.

"Let no one go too far with you," said Joachim, fixing Jack with his black eyes.

"I will only do as you do," answered the boy.

The Wrong Price

The next day Jack prepared himself. He stood on the weighing-house floor with arms outstretched, a weight in either hand. He learnt to judge the weights by feeling. But in the evening he faced the wrath of people coming to sell their flour or buy the grain.

"What use is it to have the mill working again," complained one man, "when the price we get for the flour is so small?"

Jack changed the weights in the hope that the bucket would not rise so quickly. But up it came almost before he had moved his hand.

"I'm sorry," he said but the man merely scowled and turned away with his meagre handful of coins.

"You should know better," scolded a woman. "Don't you know you give the wrong price?"

"I do what Joachim tells me," spoke Jack.

"There's trade for you!" mocked the woman.

Jack felt guilty but could do nothing.

He nearly collapsed with shame when the bucket for people buying the grain refused to rise altogether. He placed more and more weights on the scales but nothing happened. At last it lifted slightly. The price they paid was enormous. Jack was scared for his life.

When Joachim came back to check the work he found everything in order.

"Have you learnt to handle the weights then?" he asked.

Jack did not know how to reply. He felt wretched.

What You Give and What You Get

Now Jack could not remember anyone he loved. He cursed

the mill they spoke of for starting again—he did not know how. His three companions always stayed nearby, outside the weighing house, Jack knew. To sell or to buy, they all had to come here.

Then in his mind a glimmer shone, that drew him to it. A book, a cup, a knife and fork—whose things were they? For Jack could scarcely write, he never used a knife and fork and any object served him for a cup.

He felt the weights and knew that they were wrong. Some were hollow, some were lined with lead. No matter how much grain the people bought or sold they would always pay too much and come away with little.

Jack changed the weights and switched the buckets and people went away with smiling faces, brightened. The sober lines of men and women stretching out the door grew festive, merry. Jack's three companions stood in the shadows, watching.

Joachim came back at midnight. He glared at Jack.

"What you give and what you get are firmly marked inside those bins," he said, pointing at the buckets. "If you exceed those marks you break the law of the weighing-house. Beware."

Jack woke quite sick on his bed of straw. He could not feel his hands, his fingertips were numb and his eyes swam. He had nothing left that was his in the world. The cold lap of water had washed away all memory of dog or home. He walked away from the weighing-house. He left it far behind. With every step his brightness came back.

Almost as if they slid out of the sunlight, his three shadows returned.

"You have something that is ours," said the first.

"What do I have?" asked Jack in reply.

"The gold," said the second.

"You are walking away with the gold," chimed in the third.

They looked in his bag.

"There's only bread in there," said Jack.

The first man picked out a handful of coins.

"The bread has multiplied," he said.

Joachim

They led Jack to an enormous building that stood behind the weighing-house. Jack was amazed he had not seen it before. Inside, grain sighed and whispered as it slid down slopes and mountains of corn. Before Jack's very eyes the grain changed into gold and back again.

In the centre of the hall stood Joachim, his black hair tumbling down to his shoulders, and in a black robe, like an officiating priest or judge.

"You have fixed the scales," he said, "and taken the proceeds for yourself."

Jack fell speechlesss.

"Imprison him," said the first of the three men.

"Lest he speak," said the second.

"For we are secrets and may not be told," uttered the third.

"The weighing-house on the river," went on Joachim,

"deals only with correct amounts. People come to buy the value of the corn, but what they take away is what they bring."

The grainstore spun around him. Jack closed his eyes. He felt the bristly horsehair shirt on his chest. He heard a dog bark in the far distance. Who were these three men? The question throbbed in the back of his head like a dull ache.

"Take him to the prison-house," said Joachim and they led him away.

What Miter Did

When Jack had flowed with the river, and its dark currents had dressed him in this horsehair shirt, Miter the dog, in his coat of fluffed-up black, endured the minutes and hours philosophically. Some half-formed memory led him into the forest. A friendly voice, a feeding hand—there might be some comfort there.

In the forest Miter found, once more, the beginning of things, the White Rider himself. His horse stood in a forest brake, the Rider sat beneath a tree. Miter rested his chin on the White Rider's knees. The dog's eyes closed in bliss.

"Miter, my friend," said the Rider, "your master is in trouble and needs our help."

He took out a box and wrapped it in a white cloth.

"Take this to him. Tell him Miter found it in the forest—a good dog who knows where to turn for help!" And silently he was gone.

Jack, who had never heard of praying, did not know who to ask for help. Then like a dreamer waking from a dream he looked up and saw a small dog sniffing at the bars of the half-window up at the level of the street. The dog held something in its mouth white as an angel's wing.

"Miter," said the boy and it was like the sound of sweetest song. All the clouds of forgetfulness rolled away. In his heart was a cry for justice but he did not know what justice was. He shook out the white cloth.

"My shirt!" he cried, and a small box tumbled to the floor. At the same moment the door swung open and Jack heard a voice, like three voices in one, declare:

"Your crimes have been recorded. You will be held in captivity and will remain in the prison for as long as the time served by whatever man has been there longest. If it be two years, you will stay for two years, if it be more, you will stay for more. So be it! Be thankful for the mercy of the court!"

And the door banged shut.

Chapter Seven—The Scales of Truth

Amy had remembered him by now, Jack thought.

He had no other light down here.

Yet soon he reached into the gloom and saw, with searching eyes. Minute reflections—edges of metal, glistening stone, eyes. A murmur of voices. A smell of being forgotten.

It was inhabited darkness.

"You are young," said a voice, and Jack looked down. Almost at his feet lay a man with a blanket heaped round him, against the wall. "Why are you here?"

Jack put it into words as well as he could.

"Your crime is not sizing people up," observed the man. "Some men in here have killed for almost nothing, burned down homes and stolen from their friends. But if you ask them what they've done, they will all say the same: nothing."

Jack studied his dark eyes and scarred face.

"Yes," said the man, "I am honest too."

Jack clutched his bundle—the little box—in a fold in his shirt.

There were no corridors down here—every place led to every other place. Jack saw people who had stopped being human there—or had they? The light had gone out of their eyes, they jerked their hands and nodded their heads. There were the creeping ones, whose spines were never straight, and the crowing ones, whose wits were lost in a jumble of sounds.

When these unfortunates had passed, Jack saw a man sitting cross-legged on the floor. He had clear eyes, long hair and beard, and something which had been destroyed in the others: intelligence.

"There is no justice," said this man, "only the things people do to each other."

"Are you wiser than them?" asked Jack.

"Whatever you need to know, come to me—I will tell you," answered the man.

Jack felt the little box in the fold of his shirt move.

"What is the longest time someone has stayed here?" he asked.

"A lifetime," said the man. "But look at them—there are so many different lifetimes here. If you think—like me—you learn there is no beginning and no end."

"Why are you here?"

"I saw that people had forgotten how to think, how to learn, how to live by the truth. So I helped them die."

"You killed them?"

"I showed them a better way."

The box in Jack's shirt trembled, and he did too. Was he speaking to a wise man or a murderer?

"I helped them see the light," the man went on. "I can help

you too."

Jack backed off. His eyes began to blur and his heart beat fast. The little box beat against his stomach. He opened the lid and looked inside. He saw a tiny pair of scales, mounted on a stand. A little motif was written on the stand. It said: SCALES OF TRUTH. Jack shut the lid. He knew at once the scales would sink to one side or the other when the truth was not being spoken. He knew at once the scales had come from the White Rider. He could think no other.

"Miter," he spoke, into the shadows, and wondered how his dog would flourish.

He had his own two eyes to help him here, and the scales to tell between truth and fiction. He saw that people made their own prisons by the way they lived. The pulse of life quickened in him and he knew he could be free.

One Drop of Oil

The little fulcrum of the scales was stiff: it needed oil. Just one drop would do. To find a drop of oil became Jack's mission.

A rat bit him in the arm before he could start. Then he saw how many rats were running about in the dungeon. He gripped his arm. Big ones, small ones, male and female ones, mothers and grandfathers: there were more rats in here than there were people. Jack, in his freedom, had not been scared of rats, and Miter had always kept them away.

Now the little scales seemed to act like a compass, trying

to pull Jack across the floor. The tiny balances fluttered and Jack lined them up with a point near the door.

It was like a little harbour in the darkness. A point of light, a candle, lit the entrance. Within the space, like ropes on a quayside, lay silvery lengths of wire and a man whose nimble fingers twisted it into coils and loops and springs. Each small creation was tapped into a piece of wood with metal staples and a light hammer. Then Jack saw what the man was making: rat-traps.

"Gervase the trumpet-player," said the man. "That is my name. But mostly I fix things for a living. What are you?"

"I'm Jack," replied the boy.

"Are you Jack the horse-thief? I knew of a boy called that."

"I led the horse away," answered Jack. "It had nothing to do. Amy needed it."

"Well," said Gervase, "I'm not against things working. My rat-traps work a treat."

His small eyes looked up under the peak of his hat. He folded his hands over his great round belly.

"Amy..." he mused. "Amy is as Amy does."

"What do you mean?"

"You fetched her the horse. Does Amy know you are here?"

"I don't think she's forgotten me," answered Jack truthfully.

"That is a help," said Gervase. "A powerful help. Now I see you are a man who takes things as you find them. How do you find me?"

"I think you are a musical man," said Jack.

"Ah! A silvery trumpet-player I am. I used to charm the birds from the trees with my trumpet-playing. But now for my sins I'm an engineer in gaol, making rat-traps for the guards. In return they give me extra food. You can see I'm not exactly starving!" He patted his stomach.

Jack looked closely at Gervase.

"You want to know why I'm here." His eyes narrowed down. A strange gleam came into them. "It was an accident. I put down poison for the rats and someone ate it. A peculiar mistake. Not everyone liked my trumpet-playing you see."

Jack's scales wobbled again. He tried to make sense of what Gervase had said. Someone had died of poison who didn't like the trumpet-playing. Was it murder?

"An accident," repeated Gervase. "For a punishment they took my trumpet away. Now tell me what you've got there."

Jack produced the scales. Gervase studied them and sighed.

"My music was so beautiful," he said. "I'd stop eating, you know, I'd starve myself, if only they'd give me my trumpet back!" He touched one of the balances with a stubby finger. "They don't move. You need to oil the pin. I have oil here." He brought out a little can then stopped and looked at Jack. "How important is it to you?"

Jack's face glowed in the candlelight. "I owe it to Amy and Miter," he said.

"Who is Miter?"

"My dog."

"Ah! I'll help you then. A drop of oil in return for—what shall we say?—three day's work. Every commodity is valuable here."

Jack happily agreed.

Working for Gervase

He worked with the sound of invisible trumpets playing in his ears for three days. He prepared the tallow Gervase needed for his candles, and trimmed the wicks. He turned the wire while Gervase moulded its coils. He lived in a realm of sorrows and joys as Gervase told his tales.

At last a fleet of rat-traps stood ready.

Gervase was pleased. His round face shone in the candlelight.

"A drop of oil," he said, "for Amy and Miter."

Jack's heart leapt when the globule of oil touched the fulcrum of the scales. This tiny point was like the bridge between two worlds.

Now Jack heard the clear echo of murder in many people's hearts. He knew with a shock that the three men who had falsely accused him of stealing the gold were the three brothers of Joan the miller and had killed her husband. His mind, his hand, his heart reached up to the White Rider, who had made the world. He heard his name being called, "Jack," and knew that he had a home, unlike any he had known.

The scales seemed to hover in space in front of Jack even when he was not holding them. He heard the music of them; chords, he understood, which echoed in himself. A very subtle hand had made them.

Jack began to feel he knew the shades of truth with or without the scales. He questioned people openly about how long they had been there. The sight of the boy with the curly hair became familiar to them all. They took him for a fool or shook their heads but never did him harm.

Two Men

There was one wall in particular Jack came back to again and again. It was built as if it blocked an ancient passageway. He came there in the evenings and left his little bundle in the corner he had made his own.

He saw a figure one evening, crouching by the wall. His hair and beard were grey, his clothes were rags. On his face he wore a look of patience, which moved in turns towards despair and hope.

"Haste, haste," said the man, "the time is short, the way is long."

"Where are you going?" asked Jack.

"This very night I will be at home."

"Are you leaving?" enquired Jack in wonderment.

"I am turning the corner—after twenty-four years."

"Is that—is that how long you've been here?"

"Every minute of it."

"Then that is how long I must stay." He remembered his doom, that he must spend as much time in the dungeon as the person who had been there longest. He had not met anyone who had been there longer than this man.

"You need not stay that long," said the man. "We leave tonight at twelve. You are the help I need. Come with me."

Jack had left his scales behind and could not judge if the man was mad.

"The tunnel lies behind us," went on the man. "Be there tonight." And he turned away, leaving Jack on his own.

Almost immediately a second man appeared from the shadows on the other side.

"After twenty-four years," he remarked, "you will look like that too. Beware of appearances."

Jack was astonished, not by the thought of himself in twenty-four years, but by the fact that this second man was almost identical to the first. He spoke in the same way, he dragged his leg heavily as the other had done, his beard and hair had once been dark and thick but now had the evening greyness of stone.

"It is *my* tunnel," went on the man. "I have been digging it every night. I have finally turned the corner into the passageway. You can help me if you like. Come here at midnight. Be ready to fight, for the man you saw there is my enemy."

Now this second man left and Jack doubted if there was solid truth anywhere here.

Midnight

The thought of escape was like a shaft of light for the boy. The noble sun was the home of all things. It lay disguised even in the deepest places, in the dungeon or in the hearts of cruel men. Jack could escape into sunlight again but the riddle was: which man to trust?

He took the scales from their hiding-place. He knew that at the midnight hour he could not use them. He thought he was being weighed himself. The minutes grew into hours and the hours, in the hands of darkness, weighed heavy.

The first man was already there when Jack approached at midnight.

"How long I have been kept away from the light of the sun!" he exclaimed.

The second man appeared from the shadows.

"My home and family have become like a foreign land to me!" he said.

They cast a look at each other and the glance was like a clash of cymbals in that still and deadened air.

"One glimpse of sun," repeated the first man, "is all I need."

"To speak to my family and friends once more," said the second.

And Jack gazed in awe as the coal of their eyes burned into each other.

As if the reality of the wall belonged to nothing except

time, the two men worked away the stones in separate places and came through to the open air of a passageway. Jack heard the tinkling of hope and light as he passed through the entrance.

In an instant, he saw his twenty-four years imprisonment walking ahead of him, in the shape of the man who wanted light and the man who wanted converse with his family. But one of these men was a liar—or both. Which one should he stay with? He trusted his heart and followed the first man, who had wanted a glimpse of sunlight. Both men walked with a limp from an old wound, both sought the way ahead and carried a small light. Jack's scales were packed on his back and he dared not take them out. But something told him to keep to the right, where the first man walked.

The passage contained shackles and bones. Some leg-irons still contained their legs—shin-bones and femurs.

The first man looked down and shook his head.

"You see my own condition there," he said. "For twelve years I was restrained by shackles such as that."

"What was your crime?" asked Jack, unable to stop himself.

The man peered long into Jack's eyes. "My crime was to protect someone from harm."

"He says exactly what happened to me," put in the second man unexpectedly.

"No," responded the first, "your crime was that you did not prevent me."

"Decide who you will go with now," went on the other

man to Jack. "But be advised—whatever this man says, the opposite is the truth."

Jack thought. "I also want a glimpse of light," he said.

"You've been warned," replied the man. "Take care." And he disappeared off down a branch of the passageway that led in a different direction.

"Follow me," said the first man, still looking curiously into Jack's eyes.

Not a draught of air came down to meet them. A terrible apprehension came over Jack's mind that he had chosen wrongly. He started to take the little bag off his back, the bundle he had made with the scales in it.

"I would leave that where it is, if I were you," remarked his guide.

Jack swallowed hard. "Why?" he asked in a small voice.

"There is someone who would kill for what you have there."

"Who..?" started the boy in alarm.

"Who do you think? There is only one other."

Jack swung round. The second man had gone down the other branch of the passageway. Or had he? He stooped and picked up a shackle. At least he could defend himself if need be.

A Glimpse of Sunlight

Jack realized he was hearing something like the sound he heard when Amy passed through the wall of the Black

Rider's castle. It answered a longing in him. He felt, as well, very close to the unicorn boy, whom he had met so briefly—although he could not say why. He now believed quite firmly that the man going ahead of him would lead him to safety.

His love of sunlight led this solitary figure on, past fallen stones, nests of rats and crumbling bones. The ghosts and nightmares of his confinement might have risen to affright him but he would not have been deterred. Jack hopped behind, picking his path through death and evil.

Suddenly, without warning, the second man returned—Jack hardly knew where he appeared from—and raised a stone to bring down on the first man's head.

"No!" cried the boy, and his guide turned enough that the blow caught him on the side of the head rather than on the crown. The second man pulled round and reached as if to grab Jack's bundle. Jack saw the animal cunning in his eyes. He flailed with the shackle that still lay in his hand. He did not know where the metal struck, but heard a yowl of pain and, a moment later, where his attacker had stood there was now only empty air.

"Drag me to the gate," said the hurt man. "I cannot move."

Jack looked up. The gate? Was there an exit, an entrance—a way in or out?

"It lies ahead," went on the man. "A short way."

Jack raised him by the shoulders. "Don't be afraid of hurting me," he said. "The numbness has spread through my whole body." The blood trickled down from the wound in his head.

Jack inched his friend and guide towards the end of the passageway. Where the gate should have been, a cascade of stones had tumbled in.

"Clear them," whispered the man.

Jack picked out the stones and cast them aside. He worked as fast as he could. But the speed he worked at was matched by the speed with which the man was fading.

He reached through to a filling of small stones and scrabbled at them with his fingers. He believed he had failed but then, as if in answer to his clawing, he heard a scratching on the other side.

"Is someone coming to meet me?" he asked himself and looked round again for any sign of the other man. "He can't be out there and we are still here."

Now he heard a panting through the thin partition of stone. He flung aside the clay and gravel, the boulders and the small stones. His fingers were cut and raw. The gateway opened! At least a narrow hole appeared. A small black nose thrust through. Jack enlarged the hole. A head emerged, with curly hair, a panting tongue and large dark eyes.

"Miter!" cried Jack, and fell upon the dog with the embrace of one who has found his dearest friend.

"Make the opening wide enough," spoke the man, and Jack saw he had a short time left.

He shovelled away the debris from the fall of stones and created a gap wide enough for a man's head and shoulders to pass through. He turned again to his friend.

"It is too late," said the man faintly, and in the increased light Jack saw how the impact of the stone had crushed the side of his head.

"I could bring you out," said the boy in a voice choking with emotion.

"No," said the man, "my imprisonment is over. But—let that large stone be moved."

Jack wheeled away a large round stone that blocked the door. A stream of sunlight filled the cave. The dying man soaked it in with his last reserves of sight. Jack knelt before him, at his feet.

"It is all I had asked for," said the man, with lips already growing cold.

Jack saw the look of bliss on his face, the resolution of hope and pain. He turned his eyes away to the outside air, to the patch of blue sky and the sound of many birds singing. After some moments he looked back and saw that the eyes of the man were no longer seeing.

Miter pressed himself in right beside his young master.

"He meant something to me, this man," said Jack, "although I hardly know what." And Miter whimpered with a dog's own understanding.

To the Garden

Miter had stayed at the half-window of the prison cell long after Jack had been taken away to the dungeon. He had in his mind the snatches of song Amy had sung when she had felt, for the first time in her life, that she might be happy. And the sound of her voice mingled with the fortunes of his master. For Miter longed to know a home again where Jack would be found. They had tried to build a willow house, they had travelled in a caravan. It was the start of a search. Now Miter wanted it to be finished. So he walked the path back to the last place he had seen Amy—the hidden garden—and watched for an opening.

Amy had drunk poison from a cup of gold. The poison had reached down into her singing heart and pushed her close to the face of the Black Rider. He sang to her in a voice that promised great possessions, homes, and riches beyond her dreams. But Amy held another picture in her heart: a little hearth, a kettle, a horsehair bed—and Jack was there as well, searching for the home he'd never had.

Just as the ivy clad the walls on the outside of the castle, so did the trailing poison of the Black Rider creep over every crack and surface on the inside. Snakes' heads hissed and curled, writhing round the poor beleaguered girl. But Amy always found the door into the garden, and the Black Rider was powerless to stop her.

In this garden there were branches of silver, branches of gold, and branches of diamond. The woman who worked there tended the fruit of every tree—and pruned and lopped the bad ones. She withered slowly, as a result of handling the springy branches. Without that she would have been as ancient as all the days of creation. Amy, she thought, was like her younger self. She tended this tree with particular care.

There was no time in this garden, as Amy knew it. There was thoughtful contemplation, there were bells in the far off distance, and slow fruits ripening.

Amy did not know herself there. Her eyes darted from flower to flower, as if drawing out the nectar that would let her live, if only for a little longer.

The woman whose garden it was smiled at the girl with the wish still alive in her heart. Wishes are like stars that set by day, but are still there, and will return when forgetfulness passes. Therefore she spoke to Amy about things that don't matter, because in all the world these are the most important.

And Amy lived, for a time each day, in that garden, with flowers like dreams in the border around her heart. Then, when her time was up, she returned, as she had to do, to the house of the Black Rider.

The door vanished behind her, and in the same moment Jack's friend had his glimpse of sunlight.

What Would Happen Next?

In some far away wood, that was everywhere, the White Rider saw the boy's head poke through the opening, followed by the black head of the dog. The golden ball he rolled in his hand could have been: the plaything of an animal like Miter or the world he had made when things began. What would happen next?

The world seemed newly made to Jack. In miniature, the beads of dew on grass and leaf shone like globes. The past was over! A new day had begun!

"Your dog has been most patiently waiting," said the old woman.

Jack gazed into her pale blue eyes. Their living colour lifted him out of the tunnel.

"Where am I?" he asked.

"A place which has had no name since time began," she replied.

Jack looked up. "These are the walls of the Black Rider's castle!" he exclaimed.

"Yes, but he does not come here. This is a place of growth and change."

"I have a friend here," said the boy. "But he is dead."

"Bring him out," said the woman. Her eyes glanced in all directions at once. "We can bury him here."

A soft breeze blew. Petals from the rose bushes passed above the grave and dropped down.

"Isn't there something you are forgetting?" asked the old woman. "Something you don't need any more."

Jack thought. Then silently he took out the scales from the little pack on his back. He laid them down on the man's body, where the hands were folded.

When the grave was filled the old woman took Jack by the arm and said, "Now I must tell you that the man you have just buried was the defender of the unicorn-boy."

"The unicorn-boy?" said Jack and his mind flashed back to the boy in the castle.

"The Hearer by the Lake was what the boy was called at that time. A unicorn will run itself into the ground if it is not watched and this man saw to it that the poor creature would last a little longer."

"How did he do that?"

"By finding shelter for it, where it could be a boy again."

Jack remembered how the unicorn had been so drawn to the caravan and the willow-shelter.

"Now the Black Rider sent a man to stop this friend of yours from doing his job. He laid a trap which meant your friend was put in prison. But the trap failed in one respect: the second man found himself in prison too. The second man taught himself to think in the same way as the first and so they became alike. But he kept his evil heart and did everything he could to stop your friend escaping."

Jack looked up. He remembered the boy saying, "There is no Amy here—only Jack." He remembered the way he looked and spoke.

"That boy was me," he said.

"If you believe in nothing else," said the woman, "believe in that."

Jack's eyes scaled the walls of the Black Rider's castle: the green ivy, the shadowy footholds, where he had climbed once before.

The old woman placed a small jar in his hands. "Take this," she said.

"What is it?"

"The attar of roses. Pour three drops into Amy's cup when she drinks and you will see what happens."

Jack looked down at Miter. "I won't leave you so long this time," he said. "And when I come back I will have Amy with me!"

Jack gripped the ivy and climbed.

Awakenings

This was now the third time Jack had climbed an ivy to reach Amy's window. He was not scared. He had been in the Black Rider's kingdom for what seemed like forever.

The gold which Mertha could not shine lay all around. Yet Jack's eyes were not attuned to these things. What he saw was one of the chests he had opened with Amy. Why did it not stand in the tower? Who had brought it here?

Amy's voice came softly from the other side of the room.

"It is a white horse, isn't it?" she was saying. "And no more than fourteen hands high?"

"It's me," said Jack, and the heart went out of him at the sight of Amy's empty eyes, her ashen face and dishevelled hair. "I have no horse."

Amy's voice quavered. "I'll never be free," she said.

Jack saw that his friend was like an empty cup drained of

goodness. She could not see the colour of Jack's eyes or the determination he felt. She did not know him.

Jack's feet led him through the maze of goblets and platters lining the floor and tables of that room. He raised the lid of the chest. One single cup was all that remained in it. He lifted it out, being careful not to spill the liquid it contained. He placed the cup in Amy's hands. The little flask he had received from the old woman was hanging round his neck. Now lifting it over his head, he removed the stopper and let three drops fall into the juice.

"Lift the cup, Amy," said the boy who had lost his friend.

The cup moved in her hands. The slight turning awoke something in her fingers and palms. Amy drank.

As the dawn light passes over a rose, brightening first the outermost petals and then the deeper colour at the heart of the flower, so did the light of recognition cross Amy's face, until at last it filled every part of her. The liquid in the cup, tinctured with the perfume she herself had helped to collect, had done this.

It was with a whisper that Amy said, "Jack". And her eyes spoke the name again, if it is true that eyes have words to tell. No snow falls more lightly than this way of speaking, when forgetfulness ends and the world is reborn.

Jack was quite an unschooled boy who felt only joy when a friend spoke his name. He clasped his arms round Amy and hugged her as if his own dear soul had been restored.

Chapter Eight—The Book of Jack and Amy

Meanwhile, Miter, the friendly soul, made conference with another old acquaintance: a horse named Daybreak, who, by means of a path known only to herself, came near to the castle of the Black Rider. Horses are affectionate with animals lower than themselves, and Daybreak almost called out Miter's name in welcome recognition—except that words do not come easily to horses' lips. Miter's eyes twinkled brightly at the sight of the white horse trotting through the undergrowth. With barks and whinnies, some jumping, some mane-tossing and nudging, Jack's dog and Amy's horse made friends again.

Jack climbed down the ivy and Amy, dizzy with the height, followed. Down to the level earth they came. No garden, no grave lay there. If they had left by the same window Jack would not have known it. Everything seemed changed. And on the stone wall behind him he saw two armorial shields, carved by some mason and representing, perhaps, the rule of two great kings.

The re-uniting of the friends was not long postponed. And if Daybreak nuzzled up to Amy's ear, is it any surprise that she thought the horse whispered something, with unknown words?

Their escape was longed for. Through the mould and the mulch they galloped—at least in their hearts—but in truth walked as fast as they were able, with Daybreak carrying each of them in turn, and sometimes together.

By the corner of the forest they spoke of homes and houses they had known. Amy had a strong recollection of her parents and their early home. Jack had only the tiniest spark of memory in his mind of a little house below a hill and a woman who kissed him. In the shade of a grey cliff they talked of happiness lost and happiness found. At the foot of the waterfall Amy asked Jack who had made the world like this and why. Jack told Amy the story of the White Rider. Amy said, "Jack, the unicorn-boy is right behind you." By that she meant the boy was never far away.

Daybreak listened. She knew that fine words are useless without firm footsteps. And if Amy and Jack had looked round they might have seen the print of heels and toes in the soft earth. For Daybreak's steps were taught by the White Rider. His mind was in them and the shape of the footfall was his.

Dilemmas

Their journey led up through the forest in a landscape of gushing water and deep-drinking trees. Abruptly before them, as if it had been painted into the scenery, they saw their brightly-coloured gypsy caravan. And then, turning their gaze, they saw the same chest they had found just recently in the Black Rider's castle. A perilous ravine stood between them and the caravan. A further ravine separated them from the chest. There was no room for manoeuvre. Daybreak stopped and let her burden down.

The ravine struck silence into them. Then slowly Amy said, "I can only ever be a visitor to happiness. Something always has to separate me from it."

"We can cross, Amy," said Jack, "if Daybreak would jump." But Daybreak would not jump, and it was a leap too far for a horse with two children on its back.

For Amy the gap grew wider. Jack stepped towards the second ravine and regarded the chest. His mind was a turmoil of books and cups and place settings. Almost as the water of the mill pond had engulfed him he felt an inrush of purposes with no meaning.

"You must cross here," said a voice behind him, and Jack turned round expecting to see Amy. But Amy had not spoken.

"Over here!" called Jack, and he pointed to a narrow pine tree lying beside a stream. "We can lift or drag this tree and let it fall across the gap."

"What good will that do?" asked Amy.

"It can be our bridge."

They were able to rotate the tree on its ends and bring it to the ravine. The difficult thing was to stand it upright and let it fall.

"Why not to the caravan?" said Amy when she saw Jack's

intention.

"We can't," replied the boy. "Daybreak can't come with us."

But Amy saw immediately that the chest itself was Jack's desire. For the second time she gave up her dream of caravan-ing and followed where the troubled path led.

The Book

They crossed together. There they are now if you care to look: Jack in green and white, Amy in red, seated on the fallen tree, shuffling across for fear of the great distance down below. And when Amy was safely across Jack went back to get Miter, who could hardly contain himself with eagerness to reach the other side. It would be true to say Jack stroked Daybreak except it was the horse who rubbed her head against Jack's hand. And then, turning, Daybreak fled into the forest.

Thus Amy saw her caravan on the far side of the other ravine, and the horse that should pull it galloping off between the trees. But Amy had changed and she knew she could guide her life—and Jack's—without the help of a house on wheels.

Jack opened the chest. A single volume lay inside. It had a smooth leather skin enfolding white pages. It might be that Jack did not know what to do with it. There was food and drink in the chest too. Neither Jack not Amy wished to know where it came from—their hunger told them it was good, and they ate without pausing to speak.

Amy looked at the way her friend sat with the book beside him.

"Jack," she said when they were finished, "that book is meant for you."

Jack looked at the book as he might look at a strange, lifeless object.

"It has nothing to do with me," he said.

Amy laughed. "You have to write in it. Fill it up with your adventures. Call it the Book of Jack and Amy!"

"The Book of Jack and Amy," he repeated. "I would like to read that."

"Well, you have to write it first. Come on, Jack—so much has happened to us!"

"I—I only know a little bit of writing and a few words."

"That's all you need to start with."

"I don't have a pen."

"I do!" Amy took a pen from her pocket. "Begin with your house and then tell about mine. Put in all about Miter and Daybreak and the willow shelter. I'll build a fire."

Jack started to write. It felt very strange to him: "Once there was a boy called Jack. He had no parents. He had no home…" This seemed enough to Jack but then he saw Amy looking at him and thought he had better go on: "But he did have a place of his own—in a wooden box." Did it really matter if nobody knew why he was there? But it was a wonderful house, more than a wooden box. It opened into a burrow in the ground and Jack had made his kingdom there.

All the world might be cold and grey but Jack had his home and no one need tell him there was something wrong with him or the way he lived! Miter understood.

Jack looked up. Amy was lighting her fire and watching him out of the corner of her eye. He had already written nearly a page.

"Amy wanted a horse. She wanted to escape." Her uncle did not love her. Escape—real escape—sent a shiver down Jack's spine. It meant going back to what you had never had. It meant more than leaving home, more than taking your home with you. This book made Jack's eyes fill with tears.

"I can help you," said the girl. "You helped me cross the ravine."

Amy knew what Jack had written. She felt the leaving of home as a relief but did not know how to be homeless. She had lived in Jack's burrow—for a night; she had put up the willow shelter he created; she had slept in the caravan. Amy thought about it. She had her mind back and that was like a home to her.

A half-light from the moon and stars lit their words. It coloured in the edges of the chasm they had crossed and the other—the one that separated them from their former home. By midnight they lay sleeping, the fire reduced to embers. In the woods across the way a shy white muzzle appeared—and disappeared again, a horn of silver on its brow.

Dissolving

The unicorn was again attracted by the caravan. He came up to the edge of the ravine. He tossed his head and whispered in that half-language unicorns favour, which carries distant echoes of the sea and of woodlands redolent with strange creatures. With one leap he was over—a distance that poor Daybreak could not span—and penetrating the caravan. I do not think that unicorn would have pulled it but he loved to be a passenger. And while he was there the story of the White Rider was there with him, for he was the messenger of it, the Hearer by the Lake, who had become enchanted.

In that moment Miter the dog woke from sleep and raised his head. He walked the short distance to the ravine's edge and gazed at the caravan. He felt the world turning under his feet and the timeless story being told again. Miter believed Jack was in the caravan. A wonderful thing happened then: the caravan dissolved away as if it had been absorbed into the figure inside, and the unicorn stood there, very still, with a new light in his eyes.

In the morning the unicorn-boy remained as a thought in Jack's mind. Miter barked jubilantly. Amy exclaimed, "Oh look! The caravan's gone!"

Like a door opening outside of himself, Jack saw a way ahead. And in his mind's eye he saw a gypsy caravan trundling through the forest, with a boy sitting in the open doorway at the back.

"That way!" he cried and pointed to an avenue that might

once have been a path but was now strewn with fallen branches, decaying and covered with years of moss. The path led down to the sea.

Chapter Nine—A Sea Voyage

The sea itself was an adventure—cold and stirring. Countless fish abounded there who knew its depth and content, its white-flecked pages, its sentences of storm and evenings of peace. Creatures who took months to grow their shells around them heard the lapping, the ebb and flow, the moon-pulled currents. Seals, mournful-eyed, foretold the fate of many sailors, who would learn the name and nature of that country under wave. Oh, we love the sea like nothing else, and forests and high ground are well behind us!

There are names of ships which tell us everything we need to know: 'Heart of Oak', 'Conquest', 'Might and Main'. These three have been victors over mighty waves, sail-splitting winds and—retching travellers whose moans nearly reach up to the mast-head. Sail away! It is a bright morning that calls you to the ocean's swell!

Jack and Amy rose through woodland heights and dipped past wetlands teeming with birds. Heron and geese gave way to the shrill cry of gulls, each one wanting its pick of flesh from the sea.

Amy felt the lure of faraway places and wanted to reach

beyond anything she had ever known. Jack believed he carried the here-and-now under his arm, in this book—yet he had pages to fill and ways to go.

They arrived at a gravel beach. A longboat was ferrying passengers to a white-sailed ship anchored in the bay. There were chests and sacks, barrels and provisions stacked on the shore waiting for embarkation.

"Where are you going?" said Jack to a man who stood gazing out at the ship.

"To the Port of the Comrades," came the reply.

"Where is that?" asked Amy.

"It is that place to which everything of great value and beauty must eventually find its way. It rests, like a pearl in a shell, some distance from here. I am going to share my arts and crafts with the traders who live there. You see a life's work in these bags here. Yet it is nothing compared to the beauty and skill of their work."

"I mean to go there too," said Amy. She turned to Jack. "Will you come?"

Jack studied the ship in the bay. He thought of beautiful things. A feeling of hope stirred in his breast, like the flutter of a dove's wing.

"Shall we go?" he said to Miter.

"Woof!" replied the dog.

"Miter says 'yes'!"

"Then that's agreed!" laughed Amy in delight.

A Familiar Face

Jack and Amy sailed with the man, whose name was Althos, to the great ship harboured in the bay. Althos carried with him an aura of peace. He wore a long robe of an orange colour and spoke softly. He introduced them to the ship's master. The captain in no way refused their service but willingly took them on board. Their tasks were: to stitch sails, clean cabins and serve in the galley. Miter was employed as ship's dog, with special responsibility for clearing rats from the hold.

In the evenings, when the sun mapped out their course, Jack and Amy repaired sails on the deck. Glancing across to the far side of the ship Jack noticed a grey head that looked strangely familiar. When he caught a glimpse of the face he knew exactly who it was: the man who had escaped from the dungeon; the second man, who had killed Jack's friend and guide.

Jack trembled and drew into himself. Amy looked around to see what had caused his fright. She saw the man on the other side of the deck. She knew who it was because Jack had told her the story of how he had escaped from the dungeon.

Now this man had gathered around himself a group of like-minded men who were intent on doing harm. Meanwhile, on Jack and Amy's side of the ship, Althos and his company of good-hearted craftsmen and pilgrims shared their hopes and dreams about the fabled Port of the

Comrades.

On the sixth day of their journey this man Flot—for so he called himself—tied the corner of a large sail by rope to the yard arm, stood before it and summoned his men to him. He issued them with cutlasses, knives and firearms he had kept hidden in the sail. He glared across at the little group of peaceful travellers on the other side of the deck.

"Your goods are forfeit!" he cried. "We are taking charge of the ship and everything on it! Prepare to die!"

With these words he put the fear of death into the traders, who sincerely thought their end had come. However, it was not Flot's intention to kill them but to put them into such a state of terror that he could rule over them as he pleased.

Althos spoke to Flot in a calm and noble manner.

"Sir," he began, "we are all servants of each other on board this ship. Every man or woman is a member of crew as well as a passenger and will perform any task that is needed. If there is anything you want you need only ask and we will give it to you. Even the whole of our goods we will give you. The sole purpose of our voyage is to trade and admire things of beauty. Our destination is the very home of art and craft. I beg you to put down your weapons and be at peace. We are your friends and bear you no ill will."

A mighty peal of thunder rumbled above the ship immediately Althos had finished speaking. Each person there put his own interpretation on this. Jack imagined it was the Black Rider and the White Rider clashing in combat, like two knights in a joust.

The brows of the man Flot were as black as thunderclouds. He cast a particularly malevolent eye on Jack and said, "I know you from somewhere." Then he turned his attention back to Althos.

"You are just the kind of fellow I like," he said, pressing his face close to that of the other man. "The kind who says we are all there to help each other—and then helps himself. I spent twenty years in jail because of men like you. This time I won't be fooled!"

He called out behind him, "Are the captain and the crew tied fast?"

"Every one of them!" came the reply.

Flot strode around on the deck looking out on all sides.

"There!" he cried. "Black Rock! Our route goes past it. A low, flat rock with no light to mark it. Many ships have foundered here. Lower the boat!"

He led Althos to the long boat and told him to climb down.

"Take him to that rock and leave him there!" he commanded his men. And to all the good folk gathered on the side where Jack and Amy sat he said, "At the first storm that rises that rock is washed by waves. Anything on it is swept into the sea. It might be days hence or it might be this very night. Your friend can take his words more seriously there."

The thunder crashed again and lightning lit up the sky. Jack and Amy watched as Althos—now sitting, now standing—in the long boat, crossed the choppy waters to Black Rock. His orange robe shone against the darkness of the sea.

When they reached the rock Flot's men left the prisoner there and turned the boat around.

Though he sat on the highest point of the rock the waves were already casting their spray over the lonely figure. The ship continued on its way, the passengers powerless to influence the course of events. Jack felt sick to the pit of his stomach.

Black Rock

At the close of the day, at a time when the captain and his crew had previously knelt together in prayer, the former prisoner Flot came with his bowl of food and sat down directly opposite Jack.

"Your friend in the dungeon," he began, "was there just a few days longer than me."

"He is home again now," replied Jack.

"Home? His skull is crushed in."

Jack said nothing further but just looked into the man's eyes.

"Why do you look at me like that?" snarled Flot.

Jack could do nothing. His only power lay in words.

"You are going to turn the ship around," said the boy.

"Why should I do that?"

"To rescue the man on the rock."

"Are you mad!?"

Jack took strength from his book.

"You're lost," he said. "There's no power on earth that can

save you—except yourself."

Flot drew his knife.

"Explain yourself," he said, "or you are going the same way as your friend!"

"He only wanted a glimpse of sunlight. He had that. You wanted your family and friends. Where are they?"

"You ask me things you have no right to know. But I will tell you—then I will decide whether I should kill you."

He finished chewing his food and put down the bowl.

"Listen to me and I will tell you the way of the world."

Flot's Story

"When I was young I had my home in a green valley. By the sweat of my brow I made myself a place to live. It was a rich land, a good land. I put up the house myself and turned over the earth for planting. I lived between neighbours who owned adjoining territories. You never heard such people for pious words! Goodness overflowed from them—if you would believe what they themselves said. In a short time my land was the most fertile in the whole region, with fresh green shoots of corn springing up. I was married and had children. But by night my neighbours—who were such good folk—conspired to take my land for themselves. They plotted and schemed, they drew up documents to prove that my farm belonged to them, by an ancient law. Their plan succeeded and the bailiffs came to throw me out. These good people—my neighbours—stood behind them and barely concealed their glee. In a rage I went to them and lashed out with my fists, laying low first the one and then the other. My fury was so great that I did not know what I was doing. But it was clear that at least one of them would not get up again. I fled the land. I could not feel sorry for what I had done; my hatred grew and grew. I served a different master after that time. At last they put me into prison and as you know I stayed there for twenty-four years. My wife and children have long since gone. What lesson do you learn from people who proclaim their goodness then take from you what is yours? Why do you think I left that man on the rock? Exactly because he is one of them."

Flot paused. Jack spoke softly, "I know who you served."

"You know? Then you know why I killed your friend in the dungeon. You know why your scales roused my fury. Now all that is finished."

He rubbed his brow.

"Read to me boy," he said. "My head hurts with this thunder and darkness."

Home

All this time Amy had been sitting not far off, behind the coiled ropes, trying to send strength to Jack. Now she watched as he opened his book and read the words they had written together. He read of the murder that took place outside the mill and of how he himself had dived down into the bubbling water to release the stone. He read of the injustice in the weighing house and how Jack came to be in the prison. And when he read of Amy's enchantment and how the spell was broken, Flot looked up. There was a terrible sweat on his brow. The lightning and thunder seemed to be struggling inside him.

"I want my family and home again!" he cried between clenched teeth. "But they are gone forever!"

"There is only one way to find them again!" urged Jack, as if reading a script from his book which had not been written yet. "Go back to the rock washed by waves and set free your enemy!"

Flot drew near to Jack and held the point of his knife at his throat. Amy held her breath in fear.

"You speak like a fool and a madman," said Flot. "But for that very reason I will do as you say."

Now Flot ordered the ship to be turned. The evening light lay in pools on the surface of the sea. The day seemed to be prolonged beyond its course. A backing wind picked up behind them and the ship flew to Black Rock.

"Lower the boat!" commanded Flot, when they arrived there, and even as they did so his men muttered against him for weakening. The figure in orange clung to the rock in a desperate bid not to be washed away. The spray flicked over it and foam swept across its surface. Flot climbed into the boat, taking with him a long line of rope, which he looped around his waist.

The boat rocked backwards and forwards as Flot rowed single-handedly to the rock. The line uncoiled behind him, with its end secured to the ship.

Jack and Amy watched as Flot reached out his arm to Althos. But as he did so a current surged up from deep below the surface of the sea and capsized the boat. Flot and Althos were sucked into the whirlpool and disappeared.

The image rose up in Jack's mind of the man who had died at the exit of the dungeon. He heard a voice crying out, "Pull him in! Pull him in!" He watched as the sailors hauled in the line. The form that appeared above the water was clothed in orange.

"Where's Flot?" cried one of the men.

Jack imagined a different sort of line pulling Flot to safety. He saw him, in his mind, climbing out onto a ship's deck, smiling. He saw him reach out for the things he loved, the people he had lost.

"Flot has returned home," said Jack. But the man who stood before him was Althos.

Chapter Ten—The Port of the Comrades

"A long time ago," began Althos as they neared their journey's end, "there were seven comrades. They loved each other like brothers and if anything happened to the one then the others would save him. They were artists and shepherds but, if they wanted to, they could make the sea roll over with the power of their language, which was a gift from heaven.

"On land or over sea they brought peace with them. By the mercy of god they were joined as brothers—or friends—and their great dream was to found a kingdom in their likeness. They searched the seven seas until they found a kingdom suited to their needs. It had a ring of hills around it—seven in number—and faced into the greenest of seas. Its fine light reminded them always of their bond of friendship.

"In time the port that is named after them grew upwards from the shore to the hills. Never a palace did they build, for the brothers appeared among the people when it suited them. Under their keen eye the arrangement of the city was made. It spread like sprigs or branches on a tree, with little shelter needed from the storm. The houses themselves were the leaves and blossom with terraces to rejoice the heart.

"Now the comrades instructed the people of that town in the skills of every craft: the turning of wood, the shaping of instruments, the balance of hand-tools, the proportions of clay to water—all these riches were bestowed on them, including skill in the art of song.

"There is a legend of those times that puts it quaintly: one day a giant fish arose from the sea below the sea. It sucked into its chest the greater part of the ocean, leaving the ports stranded beside the chasm that used to be the sea. The seven brothers went down into the depths of this chasm armed with the lightest of swords and with their skill in song. When they saw the great fish, sleeping, they did not dare to puncture its sides with their swords lest the water of the ocean should come gushing out and flood the world. Therefore they serenaded it with soft songs and lullabies in the hope that the water would come out of its mouth slowly. This is what happened and gradually the ocean-bed began to fill again. However, the fish remained where it was so the brothers had to continue their song underwater until every last drop had been restored. Ever since that time the sailors of the port claim to hear the lingering strains of music from the ocean depths and say that the brothers have not quite finished their serenade.

"I cannot say whether or not this is true but it shows you why the art of song is so cherished in the Port of the Comrades. Small wonder that the seven friends were hardly seen after that time. In times of great need or inspiration one or other of them—so it is said—returns from the sea or comes down from their mountain fastness to help the people of the town. Those people are pledged to the gentle arts and as you have seen I am one—in spirit at least—with them. For the power of creation is a greater thing than the power of the sword."

Deserted

The more Althos spoke the more Jack believed he could see the seven brothers—or comrades—as if they stood on the deck of the ship before him. Amy's mind turned to the depths of the green sea. She longed to meet the men who had soothed the fish into releasing its great store of water. Meanwhile Miter had sniffed land and stood at the prow of the ship like a proud commander.

Almost as if the sunlight had formed it, and given their eyes new sight to see it, the Port of the Comrades appeared in the distance. The seven hills seemed to hold the town in their hands. And the water of the harbour, thought Amy, was as blue as the eyes of the Comrades themselves.

When they stepped from the boat not a single soul stood there to greet them.

"What can the matter be?" wondered Althos. "The quayside is deserted."

Miter was exuberant at standing on firm ground again. Amy followed him to the sheds and storerooms.

"There's nothing," she said, returning, "except a cold meal

on a plate."

Where was the life in such a great place? wondered Jack.

"Listen!" he said suddenly.

"What is it?" asked Amy.

"Singing."

Not Amy, nor Althos nor any of the traders or crew could hear what Jack had heard. But Jack's ears were better tuned for sounds that came from nowhere and he led his friends to the foot of a narrow street.

"I hear it too," cried Amy, and sure enough the sound of a woman's voice came winding down the hillside lanes and pathways.

The singing came from such a height they wondered if the woman was in the town at all. But like a silver thread the voice led them through the maze of passages and houses.

They climbed until they reached what must have been the last house in the town. At its entrance there stood a bush quite laden with red flowers. A woman stood inside gazing out over the sea. The last notes of her song died away into the golden sunlight. She turned as they came in but did not seem surprised.

"I thought there would be only children and honest traders," she said.

"Lady," started Althos, "we are looking for the people of this town. We have come to exchange our goods and perhaps to learn more of your art."

"The Port of the Comrades is in decline," replied the woman. "Not one soul of its population remains here. They have fled to the hills."

"And why is that?" asked Althos in astonishment.

"Knowledge reached the town that an invading army was on its way. When the people saw your topsails in the distance they escaped as soon as they could. The spirit of the Comrades has deserted us. Not a single man would stay and fight."

"And yet you have stayed behind?"

"My son is a fisherman. He has been to sea and has not returned. I will not leave the town until he is with me again."

"And why do you sing that song?"

"Out of sorrow that my son might be lost. And greater sorrow still that the Port of the Comrades is to be given up at the first sign of invasion."

Jack and Amy were astonished that the people had fled and Amy said so.

The woman looked at them closely. "Where are you from?" she asked.

The question struck a shaft of doubt into each of them. Jack could not easily say where he came from and Amy did not know who she belonged to. The life they had left behind was part of a different time and place.

"We are—escaping," said Amy at last.

The woman laughed. "If you are escaping here you are very welcome. My name is Marta. You can help me pass the time until my son returns. Unless you think perhaps you should escape somewhere else?"

"Oh no," said Amy, "we would like to stay."

Althos left to find the captain and crew and report to the traders what had happened.

Questions

Marta considered the children. "Since you are such homeless waifs," she said, "let me feed you."

She prepared a table for them—not forgetting Miter who had some choice cuts of fish at the door—and Amy and Jack sat down. The abyss that had opened up in Amy's mind narrowed down again. Jack was always at home with his dog but since he had met Amy he felt the currents of life moving him on. Although he did not know where he came from he began to take an interest in where he was going to.

"Who are the invaders?" he asked.

"They are people who are probably no different from you or me but they are not happy with what they've got."

"What do they not have?" asked Jack.

"Perhaps they don't have such beautiful things as we have."

"Why don't they learn to make them?"

Amy nudged her friend in the ribs. "Don't ask so many questions, Jack," she said.

"No," interrupted Marta, "he is right to ask. And you must ask too."

"Well, I would like to know," said Amy thoughtfully, "what is wrong with the people here?"

"They have loved wrongly," answered Marta.

"What does that mean?"

"It means they have loved the form of beauty itself but have forgotten the hand that made it."

"I think if they had heard of the White Rider they would know what to do," put in Jack suddenly.

"What do you know of the White Rider?" asked Marta in surprise.

"I know what I learned from the boy who had been a unicorn and from the cave of hours—the White Rider took me there himself on his horse called Courage."

"These are marvels," said Marta.

Miter came up to where the woman was sitting and lifted his front legs onto her knees.

"Miter has met him too," said Jack. "He wants to tell you that."

"Jack has written it down," added Amy. "Or rather I've helped him write it down."

"I would like to read that," said Marta.

Jack brought the book over to her. Marta carefully turned the pages. After a while she started to hum. Jack and Amy looked at each other—they remembered what Althos had said about how the people of this town could make music. The words of the book seemed to turn into song by themselves. The notes rose and fell; the far blue sea gave promise of eternity, and the red acanthus ringing the doorway reminded them of their purpose.

Marta stopped and sighed. "Words may do what swords cannot," she said.

Amy believed this and asked, "Where are your people?"

"They have taken refuge in the hills. In times gone by the seven comrades appeared there and gave instruction."

"Please, Marta, can we go there?"

"But—my son! If I leave here how will he find his way back to me?"

"If we don't go, there will be no town left to save. What will he come back to then? If you can sing to your people the way you sang to us now it might make them remember why their town is worth saving. Jack, can Marta sing from your book again in the hills?"

And as Jack saw this was the best possible thing to happen, quite soon the little group was setting off into the hills, carrying book and song in place of armour and sword.

Meanwhile out at sea a little fishing sloop was scudding and dipping before the bows of a great man-of-war.

"Remove that gadfly!" cried the captain of the ship, and a score of guns were trained on the little boat. But before they could hit their target the tiny vessel had swooped around the stern of the ship, and continued to annoy them unhindered.

In this way the single-handed fishing boat drew the mighty ship little by little off its course and delayed the invasion of the Port of the Comrades.

The captain of the little boat was Marta's son.

To the Hills

Althos and the artisans and the captain and the crew were waiting on the foreshore knowing that no deal might be struck, no goods exchanged, no coin received. The townsfolk of the Port of the Comrades had taken everything of value with them, everything of beauty. The journey seemed wasted.

Jack and Amy, however, were climbing into the high hills—past waterfalls tumbling through white rock, in green gullies. The sun was the painter, and his bright eye shone on that ring of seven hills, turning everything to art. If the traders went home empty-handed, they would still take with them great treasures, if only they gazed on the beauty of those mountains.

High in the mountain-tops, where the peaks jutted like points of a crown, the townsfolk took refuge. They made their dwellings out of rich tapestries and fabrics, they ate and drank from pottery with a golden glaze upon it. The sun, fine artist that he was, picked out every detail of their work.

Their hearts were empty.

Jack, when he reached there, thought that he might jump up and down and wave his arms in the air. Miter would do likewise. Perhaps then someone might take notice.

Instead, he went and looked at seven statues which stood in the open air not far away. He studied each face and thought he detected a living eye, a lock of hair blowing in the breeze, in one or the other. In this way Jack often saw with his imagination.

The book of Jack and Amy now seemed to grow more than it was. The lines of grey on which Jack had penned his words became lanes into a new life.

Marta and Amy exchanged glances. Marta sat on a pedestal among the statues and started to sing. Her singing was the very life of the book itself. The legends of the White Rider rose and fell on the air and Amy felt near to the way the world began.

A crowd gathered round and heard in the song something more than loss and doubt. Each note was a reassurance that the world remains whole even when your home is taken away, and that you will still be part of that world when time draws to a close.

It was a little time that dawned here, a small time, and yet it held within it a picture of the great one. The people there were able to see that picture; they wanted to lift it and carry it and make it real. They wanted to print it in their own creations.

"Listen to me well," said one of them, a potter. "There is nothing in the world as sure and certain as a thing of beauty, as this song has shown. Our town will pass away, our lives are like grass in the wind, but the eternal world looks down on us even while we work. Let us make what we can, let us be what the Comrades wanted us to be."

Now Jack thought he heard footsteps behind him, as if the statues were restless and stirring.

"Out of my own craft," went on the potter, "I shall fashion seven tableaux to depict the life and history of our town. It matters not if all is destroyed for then at least we will have returned a little of what has been given to us."

And one by one the people of this unusual town swore to create, each in his or her own craft, a true picture of what mattered to them.

To Create and Re-Create

The starry, starry sky looked down that night on many works of art begun but not yet finished. Jack wrote again, with the practised ease that belonged to his hand by now. Yet Amy always nudged his elbow when he wrote badly or forgot what came next. Marta mused on the fate of her son.

Miter drank in gulps of cool air and slept peacefully. In the middle of the night he woke up and saw, with undoubting eyes, seven figures lit by stars and moon and pacing through the sleeping company. Some figures you bark at and some you do not, and these were of the kind you allow to pass undisturbed. The little dog got up and walked among them. They appraised the potter's work and the other pieces of art that lay unfinished. Miter had no opinion. The seven comrades whispered in low voices then departed. The dog flopped down once more beside his master and made no promise to speak nor to keep quiet about what he had seen.

In the morning the potter started his work immediately. He corrected the first panel and began the second. "How did I not see," he exclaimed, "that this was wrong?" And he prepared the clay to depict a scene where the seven brothers walked freely in the still unformed streets of the city giving instruction.

Jack and Amy watched the work as it happened and sometimes they were allowed to help. Marta wrote down the music that had come into her head.

Meanwhile the little fishing boat kept within sight of the big ship but out of range. A peculiar storm unfolded in curls of cloud. These began on the slopes above the Port of the Comrades, tumbled down into the sea, picked up mass and strength and rolled out across the waves, backed by a furious wind. In this way the great ship could not make any headway at all and was pushed back by night and day into the mid-ocean. The sailors thought they heard strange dirges coming up from the depths of the sea. More than one said, "The seven brothers are singing our doom." But the commander refused to flee before the storm.

Of all the people Marta alone understood the danger which threatened them. Without the life-blood of the seven comrades beating in their ears they would all be destroyed. Their town would be lost and the unique power that had made it. It was like a light going out. Therefore she sang every day the music she had written down and when the people heard her singing they knew how much depended on their efforts.

There were items made—painting, carvings, works of craft—more perfect and priceless that anything these people had created before. The face or faces of these seven brothers appeared again and again, as the artists sought to portray once more the imagination that had invented their town. They did not know that in the night the seven comrades themselves looked on and left their admiration or their criticism like a waking dream in the morning air.

"We can save our town—we can!" said one of them, but how it would be done lay beyond the imagination of anyone there.

Is There Not One of You Who Will Fight?

The time was short and in the space of one week everything that was not completed had to be made as ready as could be. Where other races would have armed themselves and prepared for a fight, the people of the Port of the Comrades had created a complete representation of their life and history as a town. Jack felt that this would be armour enough but could not say why. The greatest work of all was the frieze of seven panels made by the potter, depicting the deeds of each of the seven brothers. Jack collected the stories and put them in his book.

At the end of the seven days the storm at sea was over. Althos, the captain, and the ship's company watched in amazement as the townsfolk returned from the mountains, carrying with them every kind of ornament and device known to human hand, but not a single weapon. And yet there was a might and power in the way they presented their work along the harbour wall.

Now out at sea the great ship, tossed on peaks and troughs of wild sea, waited for its opening. The crew feared death and doom and enchantment. All at once a deep mist settled over them, the wind drew back and the water stilled. The men on board looked up as if in expectation. A curtain of mist parted in front of them and they saw—seven stern figures, giant and powerful, staring down on the ship. There was not a man on board who did not see the same thing. Then, in almost the same moment, the ship passed through the last of the mist and there, where the figures had appeared a second before, seven majestic mountains rose up in a ring around a little town of white houses.

"The Port of the Comrades!" cried the captain, but not a sound nor a cheer answered his call.

Several different kinds of dread encountered each other on that harbour wall. The dread of death; the dread that what you have done is not good enough; the dread of powers that are greater than yourself.

Jack crouched down behind Miter and peered through the dog's black coat. In his heart he heard the voice of Marta singing.

The seven brothers held their place: in clay, in bronze, in glass, in paint. For the sailors spilling off the ship, and their colonel, the twinkling, sparkling sight, vivid with reflections and shining colours, brought to life again the seven figures looming through the mist, or the memory of voices rising from the depths of the sea. Splashed with this spray of awe or fear they crept along the quay. Their arms were locked to their sides and voices frozen silent. The great warship brooded heavily behind them but not one man had the wind of war in his lungs.

"We came to conquer and terrify," said the commander, standing before the panel made by the potter. "What do you say to that?"

"Our works speak for us," replied the potter. "Beyond that we have nothing to say."

The commander was pained to see that the work wrought by the potter was equal to the work wrought upon his men by the sights and sounds they had seen. And yet the high art of the seven brothers could not fail to overwhelm him too. He saw in front of him the power they had thought to capture for themselves—and now they too were ensnared in its charm, like birds in a net.

He shook his head. "Is there not one of you who will fight like a man for his town?" he demanded.

"I will fight you!" cried a voice. As if the swelling current had chosen that moment to lift him up, a youth appeared above the harbour wall. First head and shoulders bobbed up over the parapet, then legs and body clambered over. It was Marta's son, who had berthed his boat in the night on the far side of the quay.

"I will fight you all!" he repeated, brandishing his sword.

"It's the boy from the fishing-boat!" said one of the men who had just landed and, as if a spell had been broken, they all burst out in laughter and cheering.

"Take him!" ordered the commander, and it was not difficult for so many to overpower a boy. Then the leader of the adventurers continued his speech.

"We have come through storms to reach this place," he said, "and at times the troughs between the waves reached so deep we might have picked the treasure off the sea bed itself—or the bones. Death rattled his keys for us."

He turned to the townsfolk.

"I have heard about your seven heroes," he went on. "My men have heard of them. They think your comrades are magicians who cast spells on the sea and then loom like giants out of the mist. I will have no part of this. If you had met us with resistance we would have slain every one of you. But here I see our own thoughts made into art. The Port of the Comrades is not for our taking. You have saved yourselves."

He turned to his men again.

"You have your treasure!" he exclaimed. "One fighting man is worth more to us than all the finely-wrought gold in this place. We will take the boy!"

From where he knelt behind the dog Miter, Jack saw a tremor pass through the body of the woman Marta. The wildest look entered her eyes.

"Don't take my son!" she cried. "Leave me with the one treasure I possess—or else take my life!"

"No, mother, let me go!" shouted the son. "Look at me—I'm no artist or poet. I love the sea! I want to fight and conquer new lands. Let them take me. And I promise you that I will return one day, not as a sailor or fisherman, but as the captain of this ship!" And he cast a fiery glance at the commander.

"Very good!" smiled this man. "You will be like a son to me and I will make a great captain of you!"

Marta fell silent. She saw she had no choice but to let them have their way.

The great ship set sail again later that day and the sailors on board counted their blessings that they had escaped the magic of the seven comrades so safely.

Jack and Miter, Amy, Althos and all the crew of the other ship prepared to sail as well, having learned that trading is of less value than the creation of life. But as to that question perhaps only the White Rider, who lifted the veil from their eyes, has the right to speak.

Chapter Eleven—An Island Home

The ship travelled into the unsparing west wind. And if spring lulled them softly on one side of the ship, autumn creaked the timbers on the other.

At a certain time of life a human being must read her own seasons, and this is what Marta now did. For she determined to travel with Jack and Amy. The captain was bound for other likely ports of call.

Between the soft currents, mermaids and mermen kept pace with the vessel—at least that is what the simpler hearts believed. For what are these creatures except the good spirits which guide us through life? Jack knew this, and Miter, peering over the bows, barked excitedly at the porpoises accompanying them.

The name of the ship? Storm Rose, and its emblem a flower.

The moist air gave way to fog and fog to dense stillness. Jack was still writing in between times and Amy was talking with Marta. Their low voices—together with Jack's thoughts—wove a thread of sound, sometimes here, sometimes there around the ship. Lapping water filled in the spaces.

Marta grew thoughtful. Amy had come to admire the woman for her presence of mind and her readiness to go with them. She thought that if she could be like anyone she would choose to be like her new friend.

When Marta broke the silence it was in a voice that was neither speaking nor singing but both at once. At least so it seemed to Amy.

"There is an island near here," she said.

Jack looked up. The dense mist packed them all around.

"How do you know?" asked Amy, wondering at the special note in Marta's voice.

"Because I was born there," replied the woman.

This was a new idea to Jack and Amy.

"I am not from the Port of the Comrades," continued Marta. "I spent my earliest years on a little island far from any civilized land. My father's cottage was the only house on the whole island. He was a shepherd and farmed a few fields of crops. But the island was so lush with green grass and rich with fruit that no one need ever go hungry—man or beast. But my father and mother missed the fruits of learning and culture. They arranged for me that I should go to live with my uncle in the faraway Port of the Comrades, that I might not grow up ignorant but should learn skills and crafts. I left my home at the age of six and since that time very few ships have found their way back to the island. All contact was lost with my parents and I learned to think of my uncle's family as my own. But something deep in my childhood's soul still feels that long grass blowing in the breeze and the eternal stars circling the island. It is near me now."

A kind of excitement rippled through Amy then: a home, an island, a happy childhood. If she could return to it too she would.

The Island

The ship's bows pierced the mist. A yellow-green sunlight appeared in the heights; a green foreland, dotted with inlets and coves, stretched before the sailors' vision.

"Captain!" cried Marta, "set me down on this island!"

"There is no island on our charts!" replied the master of the ship.

"But there—you see it before you!"

"I prefer not to see it. We've lost time already. This island is uninhabited and should not be here!"

Marta turned to Jack and Amy and shook her head.

"He says it should not be here. Then I should not be here either! Captain," she went on, "if you do not set me down on this island I will jump over the side and swim!"

"If that is your wish then I will leave you here. But do not imagine I will go out of my way to return and pick you up. If we find the island again on our return journey then so be it. Otherwise—you've found your home!"

"That's exactly it," replied the woman.

"Lower a boat!" commanded the captain.

"We're coming too!" cried Amy.

And a moment later all three of them, plus Miter the dog, were crossing the narrow channel between ship and sandy cove.

A Cottage

Marta and Amy set off up the sward with one accord, leaving Jack to pull in the boat. Jack, who was a writer now, felt no such need to hurry. The world was his home and everything in it was matter for his pen. For every footprint on every island has meaning.

Jack saw his friends shake off their shoes and delight in the lush green grass. He followed them slowly. Miter ran at full tilt.

Amy and Marta were staring at a ruined cottage when Jack reached them. It was a pretty place indeed, with as many as forty different kinds of flower around it. The grass was blue with speedwell and sweet with wild thyme. But Marta and Amy stood in a place of their own. For Marta, the fallen-down walls meant loss and recovery at once, for the early years of her childhood were mingled with the stones. And Amy felt with Marta.

"This was our home," spoke the woman, touching the ruined wall with her hand.

"Did you think..?" began Amy.

"I did," replied Marta. "I thought perhaps my parents would still be here."

When Amy walked through the doorway she tried to imagine the sound of voices, the smell of cooking, the games a child might play on a cottage floor. But this floor sprouted moss and grass, and looking up Amy saw the blue sky forming the roof, with no rafters to hold it in place. Only the chimney still stood and beneath it the hearth.

"We could cook here," said the girl hopefully.

"Why not?" agreed Marta.

"If I had a long time," said Jack, "I could make a roof for this house."

"With a skylight?" suggested Amy.

"I would make it so that two whole sides could be moved and you could see the sky whenever you wanted."

"That would be just like home."

Amy swept out the ashes—as she had done once before, in the caravan—and set the fire. Marta satisfied herself there was no grave around the house and made her mind busy with how to restore the stones to their former position, and capture, if she could, some memory of the way her parents lived. Even without the timbers the building was soon homely, clean and—fragrant with the scent of open air.

Jack admired the spiders swinging away from the threat of cleaning. Like them he set his thoughts on the task of shelter. Every creature has to make its home where it can. At last he thought the canvas from the boat would do for an awning and he could, if he wished, furl it up to look at the stars. The job was soon done; a meal was cooked and happiness reigned on the cottage floor.

Amy and Marta spent the next few days absorbed in

homemaking. How a roofless cottage can be a heavenly delight! Jack, however, slept with other things under his pillow—wishes and dreams he couldn't account for. One thought carried him across the island and then another brought him back, until he felt he must know what lay in the middle. He was restless, as it were, to find out where life began.

Descendants

The thunder of the surf disturbed their sleep one night, as a rainless storm swept the island. The next morning the sun shot a ray directly through the low window, striking the boy where he lay curled beneath the awning. Neither of his companions woke but Jack arose, went out through the doorway and down to the green slopes at the end of the island. Sea, sky and land sparkled more brightly than ever.

Then Jack heard the sheep. A migrant flock had come round in the night seeking shelter. They had no shepherd. Jack decided they were descendents of the animals Marta's father once had farmed. He listened in amusement as a sturdy ewe meh-eh-ed like an old grandfather who wants his pipe—so deep was its voice—while from the other side of the crest there rose a tiny bleating, high and musical like a babbling stream. The voices grew more and more frantic as if the separated couple might never meet again, until suddenly a little lamb appeared over the hill and identified its mother by that special deep note which could not belong to anyone else.

A sudden shower of snow unseasonly swept across and when it had passed the temperature lifted. There could be no telling what time of year it was on this island. And once again the tracks which did not lead around the shore, and which the sheep had no part of, called on Jack with a strange intensity to learn what lay at the centre.

Miter had his head down a rabbit-hole. His mornings were spent in the dunes where the wind and tide washed wide the openings of many warrens. He deserted his master long enough to do his duty as a dog and then returned empty-jawed but triumphant at scaring nothing at all from its hole.

Now dog and boy returned to the house at the same moment and saw, with rising disbelief—on the boy's part at least—that the two ladies were reclaiming timbers from where they lay half-buried in the ground or on the floor of long-ruined outhouses.

"Do you mean to put up the roof?" said Jack.

"We can try," replied Marta, heaving at a beam. "At least over the chimney-place."

"And what if the ship comes?"

"There's no guarantee of that," said Amy.

"I'll help you a little."

However, house and home were two different things in Jack's mind and he kept urging his friends to explore the island with him.

"There's nothing to find, I doubt," said Marta.

"We've work to do here," said Amy.

And now again, at the end of the morning's work, Jack said, "Will you not come to the centre of the island with me?"

"The ship might come," said Amy carelessly, and Jack chose not to reply.

But Marta put down her tools and said, "The ways are tangled and overgrown; wild beasts live there—if we do not get lost we are in danger of being eaten."

At that moment a long-haired, grey cat bounded through the window opening and approached the fire where a meal was cooking. Miter, spying the intruder, barked furiously. The cat spun round, hurtled across the floor, and disappeared outside. Miter chased after it. The three human residents of the cottage followed, on the run, to see what would happen.

The cat flew across the old beams, where Marta and Amy had left them, and over the vegetable garden—as it once had been. At last it reached a high fence and, deciding not to jump, turned, with every hackle raised, to fight the dog.

But Miter, seeing the teeth and the claws, stopped in his tracks. The cat hissed and spat; the dog turned and slunk away slowly, tail between his legs.

"Well, you are no fighter of wild beasts," said Jack, arriving at that moment.

"I know that cat!" exclaimed Marta. "At least, it is identical to one I remember from when I was a girl, living here. It must be a descendant."

The cat now, at its leisure, nimbly jumped to the top of the fence, and dropped down on the other side.

"Let's see where it goes," said Amy.

They all three climbed on a gate where they could see over the fence. The cat had regained its composure and was licking its paws. But it was not still for long because a small rodent-like creature emerged from a hummock of grass and scuttled along the ground.

"It's a rat!" cried Jack.

"Or a guinea-pig," suggested Amy.

"I remember these creatures," said Marta. "It's from another old family."

The cat was on its heels immediately but the little animal slipped through a hole in a wicker fence and raced for the shelter of a box or coop which remained there from times gone by. As smooth as silk the cat leaped over the fence and, making itself as tiny as could be, squeezed into the creature's hiding-place. The animal must have made its escape another way because before long the cat appeared again, empty-handed as it were.

The three onlookers watched in fascination.

"You see?" said Jack. "That cat goes where it pleases."

"What do you mean?" asked Amy.

"I think Jack is trying to tell us something," said Marta.

"Yes," went on the boy. "It trusts to its luck—and to its skill. If it goes into a small space it knows it can get out again. It jumps fences as if they were nothing. If it meets an enemy it turns and fights. Shouldn't we be like that?"

"You want us to come with you," smiled Marta.

"I do," answered Jack. "I desperately do. Forget your work in the house for a while."

"All right, Jack, you win!" said Amy.

"You've persuaded me," said Marta.

And so an hour later they set off, with talk of cats and rats and dogs, for the heart of the island.

The Heart of the Island

What seems short in the mind wears long on the feet, and Jack did not easily unravel the different ways they might go. They could not be called paths because neither man nor beast trod them. But there were directions, so to speak, into the island, where the ground was more or less uncovered of tangle, and which were inviting enough. The difficulty for Jack lay in finding the compass hidden in himself which would lead him in the right way. Perhaps something remained in him of the scales of justice, in slightly altered from, but whatever it was a certain instinct developed in him to say, 'This way is good, that way is bad'.

Measure by measure the climate poured on them: sunshine, from the trees; mist, slipping down the mountains; cold blasts of wind from rivers; and, lastly, soft air, mild air, borne as it were by the birds and the butterflies.

Now a strange thing happened, for the wholeness of plant-life appeared before them. First, the simple root and idle stem, with little happening upon it. Then the same plants—be they trees, shrubs or flowers—showed tender buds and shoots as if spring had caught them by surprise. And a little bit further on, the same forms of life were sprouting leaves and green boughs; clearly summer was in their midst. After that, on every hand, a profusion of flowers burst out. Finally, there were trees with red fruits, green fruits, purple and blue, but not a leaf left to hide their twigs and stems. As the walk continued it was clear that all four seasons would accompany them to the heart of the island.

Jack went forward as if a sacred task had been entrusted to him. In all his short life he had not spoken to anyone who gave him such a task, but he felt it nonetheless. A voice spoke or a light went ahead of him—he could not be sure. In reality, these things were there all the time but he lost sight of them. Now his feet felt guided and he led Marta and Amy resolutely on the right path.

To rearward all was a-tangle. Who could find his way back from this temperate jungle? Soon, the colossal truth dawned on them that they were not in any world they remembered any more. Then suddenly, as if moon and sun had been cast behind them, they found themselves at the heart of the island. It was like this: a singing bird sat in a beautiful tree. Simple, but in all four travellers—Marta, Amy, Jack and Miter—the feeling arose, this is my home. Sometimes there is a person you meet who makes you feel: here I am completely understood. This tree, and the bird, and the four seasons on the tree, and the bird's delicate tune, gave each one of them this feeling. For Marta it was much greater than the memory of her parents and the cottage; for Amy the desire to live through others vanished and she knew she could have her own home; for Jack the wish to write widened into a desire to teach; and Miter, if he remembered anything, basked in the same glorious warmth he had felt from the hand of the White Rider.

It takes courage to stand before the hearth-light of your true home, and hear the songs of your life lifting in the air— just as much courage as it takes to fight like a soldier in the world. Perhaps it grows too much or becomes difficult to stay. At any rate, Jack and Amy and Marta (and Miter) were suddenly alarmed by the presence of a mountain-lion appearing on a rocky outcrop above the tree. Afterwards they had differing memories of it: did it roar, did it rear, did it sail through the air in a flying leap? It was enough for them all to flee except—Miter. This lion-hearted dog—who had quailed before the cat—now stood his ground and barked, like a lieutenant launching his troops into battle. But Miter had no troops—only himself, to hold the lion at bay. And this he did long enough for his master and friends to escape. Perhaps the lion was not used to dogs and their fury. Anyway, Miter finally scampered off through the trees and the lion retreated to its cave.

Jack awarded Miter the highest honour a dog can achieve: that is praise and affection. Their flight back through the forest was swift—indeed if they had been birds sailing the soft currents of air they might not have arrived 'home' more quickly. This had something to do with not thinking, not noticing the seasons multiplying on the trees. The tangle was a forgotten thing, just as the jungle had been un-remembered when they entered it.

And when they came to the homestead of crumbled stones and ruined sheds, it did not hold their attention for a second. The mist had returned and looming through the mist a mast and top-spar appeared for a brief moment.

"The ship!" cried Amy. "It's returned!"

Chapter Twelve—The Ship

Jack, with his steady gaze, realized at once that something was different about the vessel. Perhaps the mist magnified it—he imagined it to be the same ship grown large and pale. Only a trick of the eye could change appearances in that way.

"To the boat!" cried Marta. "You'll miss your passage home."

And in their haste Amy did not take in the choice of words.

Miter was pitched head over heels—four heels—when Jack pushed the boat off the shingle. It lurched into open water and Jack only just managed to swing his legs over the side and hop in. All thoughts were on the ship ahead and not on the experiences they had left behind.

Jack took the oars. Marta sat in the rear of the boat and, even with her island home behind her, she gazed out with a new strength and serenity. No bags nor cases to weigh down the little boat; they had an appointment with the great ship and could not delay. Amy, at the prow, called out her best directions to Jack; but the tranquil water gave no clue as to which way was the right one, and more than once the boat turned round in a complete circle.

"There!" cried Amy. "The ship was there a moment ago!"

"It's gone," said Marta. "More to the left I think."

"This mist is impossible!" went on the girl. "Turn right around, Jack, and we'll go back to where we last saw it."

"Right around left, or right around right?" asked Jack, growing confused.

"Oh, there!"

"What?"

"It's right in front of us! Look!"

Jack turned and, for a second, caught a glimpse of a mast soaring high into the air, a crow's nest perched on top, and sails furled neatly.

"It's not the same ship," said Jack.

"It must be!"

"It's not possible that two different ships would find this island in such a short space of time," was Marta's opinion. "The captain must have found his way back."

"I'm going towards it anyway," said Jack. "It's the only ship we have at the moment."

And, feeling sure he was doing the right thing, Jack struck out for the ship—or at least the place it had been a moment before.

Deserted

He rowed for what seemed like an age and half an age combined. Then, when hope had almost given out, the heavy wooden timbers of the ship appeared not six inches away from the nose of the little boat. Amy gasped, Miter fell over for a second time, and Marta stared.

"I'm not sure that you were not right," she said to Jack.

The walls of the ship towered above them, ghostly, silvery and proud in the mist.

"What now?" asked Amy.

"Shout?" suggested Jack.

But they did not need to shout, because a clambering-net was flung over the side of the ship, undraping itself to the level of the boat. And still no call or cry or echo disturbed the silence.

"I think we'll be sailing the ship ourselves," said Jack, without realizing how prophetic his words were.

"Climb," said Amy. "I'll take the book if you take the dog."

Jack tucked Miter into the sling he wore around his front and which he had been in the habit of carrying his book in, up until then. Amy found space inside her jacket for the book. Miter wriggled and was not able to make himself as small as he might have done, but dogs on the whole are not good climbers and there was no other way to get him up on the deck. Marta came third, gripping the cords less tightly than the children, but climbing very ably.

Yet when they stepped out onto the deck it was quiet as a cathedral. The shove and shout, the seaman's bragging, companionship of men—all were absent. Not a soul stirred. And yet the ship *felt* manned; in good order. If the paint was still wet Amy might have thought the ship had been refitted and the crew had gone ashore to spend their pay.

A wild voice—like the captain's but not like it—rose like a whirlwind from nowhere, sped to the fo'c'sle and issued command:

"Jack, Amy, hasten to your places—we sail on the ebb-tide!"

To Sail a Ship

Jack had seen that the tide was already beginning to ebb, for the ship baulked against its position and pulled on the anchor, like a horse chomping on the bit.

"What *are* our places?" he cried.

"Jack to the crow's nest, Amy to the wheel!" came the reply.

Jack looked up at the mast-head, which might have been a mountain pinnacle, its head couched in stars, it seemed so high above. Amy's eye dashed to the wheel and took in its wild spinning, with its grave consequences. They both had it on their tongues to say, "I can't do that!" but held the utterance back, wondering at the same time where the master of the ship had hidden himself.

Jack climbed the rigging. At a point no more than half way up a seagull approached him, eye to eye, then spun away again on upper currents of air. Higher still he thought he heard whispers and voices mingling just out of earshot, then realized that the wind was in the sails, loosening them, with many little noises. Presently the mist took him into its breast and Jack lost any feeling of a deck below. The crow's nest sailed on its own little sea of cloud, for all the world like the coracle Jack had floated in once before. Only this time he had a mighty ship beneath him—and Amy who needed his help!

Amy, in fact, listened for further command. Like a small commander herself she took the helm but could not issue instruction to her own hands. Poor in spirit was how she thought of herself then and indeed she looked like a little point of light with no means to direct its rays. Marta, meanwhile, crossed the deck from side to side looking for any member of the crew.

Then came the wind—the same wind that had turned the seasons into bran and tossed them in the air. It sheared the anchor from its rocky depths, made a funnel of the sky and poured its full strength into the sails. Jack was so buffeted for a moment he nearly lost his grip and fell from the crow's nest. The race was on!

The ship, untutored, hurtled towards the greenish sun, still peering gloomily through the mist like an old man rubbing his eyes on waking up. Then, in a moment of elation, Jack saw beyond the banks of fog into the near distance. And immediately he observed several reefs, or rings of rock, projecting away from the island. The ship could hardly fail to hit the first of these and be shredded into pieces.

"Amy, far below! Are you there?" he called in panic hardly knowing what to say.

"I'm here, Jack! I'm here!" The voice came up. "I can only

129

just hold the wheel!"

"Amy!" cried Jack again. "Port is left, starboard's right. Steer to starboard now, as hard as you can go, or we'll be dashed on the rocks!"

And Amy, though as good as blind herself with the mist still at her level, spun the wheel to the right, wrestling with it, where normally a man of three times her strength and years of practise, would control it with ease.

It seemed to Amy that the whole weight of the world lay beneath her and no hand of hers could make it turn. Always at the mercy of others, she felt little faith in her own power to determine the course of events. 'Escape' seemed like a small matter compared to this. But little by little her strength prevailed; the rudder turned; the ship hove to starboard, cutting a line through the foaming waves just as the jagged rocks might have sliced through her hull.

The first ring was passed but then the second loomed ahead impossibly close. Jack could see no way through, and then suddenly his searching eyes discovered the channel leading to the open sea through this and other barriers of rock.

"Amy! To port, to port—hurry! As hard as you can go!" he cried again. And Amy forced the wheel round to the other side with all the strength she could muster. Marta had returned to deck by this time but did not dare to break the concentration of her young friends.

For a minute the ship seemed unable to make up its mind what to do, and then at last it responded to Amy's prayers and urgings, swinging round to port. To Jack's great relief the ship slipped through the awesome jaws of rock and into the channel.

To port, to starboard, a little here, a little there, he instructed Amy, and she began to feel almost confident that she could do what he asked. The ship was learning to respond to them and it wove in an agile fashion through several more dangers, by good luck—so it seemed to Jack—missing the worst of the rocks.

And finally, with a swerve under the very knees of the wind itself, the ship passed through the serrated teeth of rock guarding the outer approaches to the island. They were high upon the open sea. Jack whooped like a mountaineer reaching the summit, and startled a passing seagull. Amy clung to the wheel exhausted and emotionally drained. And she thought to herself, "Let the crew stay away and the captain disappear, we'll manage on our own, we will!"

And now a strange sorcery occurred, because Jack saw neither land nor sea, but his vision reached to the great blue beyond, where flashes of light picked out icy mountains, frozen wastes and caves gouged out by snow. And yet on the other side, which could be neither east nor west, north nor south, but some other direction entirely, his eyes discerned steaming jungles, haughty, arid deserts throwing up glints of reflected light from the sand. How could it be that he, so high, was seeing these things, like a master of the universe peering down on the created world?

Then almost in the same moment the vision vanished, the

mist cleared, and Jack saw the island again, as if painted in the seascape by an artist with sparkling colours. White horses topped the waves all around and for a second Jack imagined he too was riding on the back of a tremendous white horse. And then he remembered one word: 'courage'.

Ironic, then, that in the moment when everything seemed to be conquered, he saw the pennant on the masthead; creeping forth like a snake from its basket it straightened and loosened itself to reveal a black motif with a silver outline against a grey background. Jack had seen the symbol before: carved in a castle wall. It was the crest of the Black Rider, and now it rode rampant atop the ship.

They had unwittingly become slaves of their enemy and had learned how to navigate his ship! Jack had plucked Amy from his very stronghold, but now the Black Rider was their master again. And yet how odd it was to be up there so high, surveying the far-flung places of creation, and all the while to be in the grip of their destroyer. How was that possible? In that moment Jack saw that it was the Black Rider's task to take the light and the intelligence out of all created things. No wonder he craved the sparkle of gold. And the unicorn-boy, the watcher by the lake, had seen it all happening. Jack felt more like this boy than ever, and began to think that perhaps they were one and the same. For now, however, he had to climb down the rigging again.

A Discovery

The ship, apparently, had not moved from the spot where it had started—or else had returned by some strange circular motion—and the ship's boat, with its oars still locked in the rowlocks, was bobbing placidly at its side. Marta was peering down, eyes fixed on the douce blue water, and listening to the gentle slap, slap of the little waves on the hull of the boat.

"I must go back," she said, "I must."

Jack was amazed. It was as if she had been there, seen what had happened, but had let it all slip away from her memory in her desire to return to the island.

"Amy," she called, "let me hug you."

Amy came down from the bridge and saw immediately that Marta had one thing only on her mind.

"I have no part in this here," she went on. "I can't leave my home a second time."

A pang shot through Amy's heart.

"Will we see you again?" she asked.

"Amy," Marta replied, "our hearts beat as one because we have been to the centre of the island together. Whatever happens, 'home' is firmly fixed inside us. It doesn't matter if we are on the island or some other place, we will still be united. But for myself I have to stay where that little hearth remains; under the open sky or covered, it matters not. And yet I think that we will see each other again, just as I know my son will sail his ship here one day and find me living among my cats and sheep and guinea-pigs!"

Amy had to laugh at this but the tears still flowed and she felt as if she were losing a mother. But, that their tasks belonged on the ship was as certain as that Marta's belonged to the island.

They said their goodbyes, Miter too jumping and barking. Marta rowed away with just one backward glance. Then Jack and Amy turned and faced each other.

"It is the Black Rider's ship," said Jack.

"I know," said Amy. "I heard his footsteps. They were the same as the ones in the castle."

They hugged each other, and felt a strange exhilaration, not quite fear and not quite hope.

A single star came out in the evening sky. A bell rang from the far end of the ship. A kind of peace fell over the vessel, with the exception of Jack and Amy's beating hearts.

"It's the time of the evening meal," said Amy, remembering the routine on board ship.

Jack took a deep breath. "Shall we go to the galley?" he asked.

Amy nodded. There was a cold, springlike air around them, holding a promise of long days to come. But they felt like they were entering a tomb as they descended to the galley.

A strange thing happened when they entered the galley, for immediately they saw not the brown, oaken walls around them, but airy spaces divided roughly in squares and reaching up to a beehive point at the top.

"It's the willow shelter you made!" cried Amy.

"*You* made it," said Jack, admiring the slender shafts of willow, uniquely knotted with twists from the same plant. The whole structure was delightfully refreshing, with tiny buds and leaves springing to life almost visibly around them. And then they felt a terrific solemnity, for there in the middle of the shelter—greatly enlarged as it was—lay the three chests from the towers in the centre of the forest. Even the smell was there: a mustiness, comprising stone and moss and—wonderment, the sensation you experience in the presence of something very old and meaningful.

"Did we make a shelter for these things?" Amy asked.

"For the old man," remembered Jack. "But now that I think of it he was a kind of custodian of the place."

"But why in the ship?" wondered Amy, gazing out. The pale blue sky dotted with stars like tiny flowers appeared through the 'walls' of the shelter.

"Perhaps we've done something we didn't know," Jack replied.

And then they heard the footsteps.

Now the silence of the tomb walled them in. All colours merged into blackness as they thought of the figure who would stand before them shortly. That they were already discovered they knew quite well, for they had sailed his ship. They had done his bidding where, to the very ends of time, they had tried to resist it before. Each step seemed to last an eternity. Neither of them dared breathe while waiting for the next. And yet they refused to go back—in their hearts they knew Amy would not live in her uncle's house as she had done before, and Jack would not dwell in innocence in his burrow. Despite the presence of the one who was almost at the door neither Jack nor Amy wanted to undo a single minute of the events leading up to this moment.

Yes, they expected blackness to enter, albeit girt with jewels, but when the door opened it was not so at all. A soft pink entered in, like the first tint of dawn on a spring day. They felt a cool breeze stir around them, as if they had slept in the willow shelter and woken to the chilly but welcome morning. They could have sworn birds were singing. And then they felt the presence before they saw the person. It was as if a smile had reached them, with no face to wear it. Miter knew who it was and barked brightly in recognition.

The White Rider had arrived.

Chapter Thirteen—The White Rider

Jack felt every colour drain out of him when the White Rider entered. And with them went the twigs and stones, the mortar and mud that had made up his life so far. It was as if a whole building had vanished and left only the idea behind it.

Amy had the feeling of gaining your balance in water, as if standing on a raft or in a small boat. And she felt all the soft currents flowing beneath her. There was music in them and love, untold, but waiting.

To see him you might have thought he was just a man; but all beginnings and all endings were tied together in him. He was like a friend and a secret at one and the same time. You felt foolish if you could not guess the answer and yet—there it was, sitting among you. You see from this how difficult it is to describe him. It is like trying to write with paint—how much better to let the paintbrush flow.

"Now," said the White Rider, "look into the chests."

Jack opened the first chest. It was the one he had seen in the third of the towers, the one filled with books. He gazed on their leather bindings, embossed with gold. The mildewed look, the mustiness had gone from them.

"Now open the second chest."

The cups were there, as before, but now gleaming with the sheen of true gold.

"And the third."

This time, when he opened the third chest, Jack discovered three place settings—knives, forks and spoons—mounted in a case of blue velvet. But there was nothing rich or ostentatious about them. Simply that they seemed to go back to a time of shared living before the world grew used to its complicated ways.

"You have learned what the books are for," said the White Rider, and his voice was like a ray of sunlight falling on the open pages. "But let them be true—for can the blue sky tell a lie?"

And Jack knew he meant that every written word must have the same truth in it that the White Rider had used when he founded the world they had come to.

"The virtue of the cups you have discovered, between you," he went on.

And Amy thought with joy how those drops distilled from the attar of roses had awakened her—but only after Jack had gone through the dungeons and terrors of forgetfulness for her sake.

"The cost of living and growing is in these drops," said the White Rider, as if reading her thoughts, "but not in the lustre of gold my brother, the Black Rider, sought to find through you."

Peace was what Amy felt then, because neither her uncle

nor the Black Rider had been able to force her to do what she did not want to do.

"But now," continued the White Rider, "I have summoned you to the galley. It was my voice you heard commanding you above deck and it was my hand which rang the bell. You are welcome to the feast!"

The White Rider moved his arm in a broad sweep from left to right and immediately the great carved table was arrayed with every kind of food and drink the children could have wished for—and after all their adventures they were longing for good things to eat and drink.

A Way In—Or a Way Out

The beginning of the meal, the continuation of the meal, and the end of the meal were, to Jack and Amy, like times past, times present and times future—and the White Rider lived in all of those. At last he spoke:

"Jack, Amy—let the cup you offer to your friends be filled always with the attar of roses, such as our mother, the lady of the rose garden, gave to you. Let the words you speak be taken from the Hearer by the Lake, who tells the truth as he has heard it. And when in your own world you dine with your guests may you know that the feast is mine and every crumb you eat is from my table."

"Are you in my world?" asked Jack.

"Jack, you have slipped out of your world for a time and found home and homes in unexpected places. A dungeon is a home; a man's longing for his silvery trumpet; a lingering gleam of sunlight. You will know what to say when the time comes—then you will see me in your world."

"But what about the Black Rider?" wondered Amy.

"Amy, my brother will always be there too. Wherever there is light he will colour it in with darkness. You must learn what can be kept away from him. There is a part of the world—your world—that can never be possessed. Remember that."

"You will always let us make our own mistakes, won't you?" said Amy.

The White Rider smiled. The world seemed to flood with sunlight.

"Every deed is a mistake as much as a truth," he replied. "It is up to you to find what remains when all the shelters are gone. Who really lives there?

"Beauty, truth and goodness are the pillars of my house. Jack, Amy, you have been denied a normal childhood. What education have you had? Leave those things to others, and let them be pleased with what they have. Think now, of the sea and of the Port of the Comrades—what you have left and what you have taken. Hurry home then, for you have more than what you need to live well. And may those who think they know better come to you and learn."

The White Rider reached up and removed a hatch directly over his head. Amy looked up and saw exactly the same view she had seen from Jack's house: the clear blue sky; shimmering sunlight. And then she knew she would go back

140

to her uncle's house—but without fear, and in freedom.

Jack did not spend much time, in his mind, on the sun and sky. The hatch for him was a way in—or a way out, he did not know which.

Jack went up first. And as he clambered through the opening his hands felt sods of earth, tufts of grass, leaves and branches. He was home again, at his shelter, but the plants had grown wild over his roof. Miter came next, springing lightly over the lid of the skylight; immediately he fell to sniffing and surveying his home ground. And, lastly, Amy herself was helped up by the White Rider; in his hands she felt transported from heaven to earth. And then out, into the daylight.

In fact, the first thing Amy said was, "Daybreak!" for there stood the white horse as if it had never moved a footstep from Jack's front door.

Chapter Fourteen—Jack and Amy

These are the days and hours of Jack and Amy: that are spent in hope, and in happiness. For their home is blessed with those pillars which make strong the house of the White Rider. His art, his truth and his virtue and theirs, while they walk in the rich avenues or down the humble pathways shaded only by leaves and ferns. The gleam of gold, so much desired by the Black Rider, is a spark you will see in the eye of a boy like Jack or a girl like Amy.

Daybreak, Miter, Amy, Jack returned to her Uncle's house. The gates were gone; the intercom exchanged for a bell. The stable stood empty.

"Look, Jack," said Amy, "we can leave Daybreak in there."

Miter dashed to the front door excitedly.

"What can he be doing?" said Jack. "No friend lives here."

But the door opened and out stepped a woman of silvery hair and kindly appearance.

"Well," said the woman stooping down and stroking the dog, "you're a friendly one!"

"Is it—?" began Amy. "Could it be?"

The woman came up to them.

"You must be Amy," she said. "I'm your uncle's sister,

Mary."

"I thought you were someone else!" exclaimed the girl in surprise.

For Mary looked so much like Marta that neither Jack nor Amy could believe it was not the same person. Even Miter seemed to need no convincing.

"You are very welcome back," smiled the woman.

"Where is my uncle?" asked Amy.

"I'm afraid to say your uncle died several months ago—in a riding accident. His horse had to be destroyed. But I see you have your own horse now."

"This is Daybreak," said Amy. "And this dog is Miter, and this"—she turned to Jack—"is my best friend Jack who will never go away from me again."

Mary listened attentively.

"I see you have been through some adventures together. Well, I know what my brother was like, and I understand why no one could find you after his death. I will not ask you to leave your friend. Do you have no home yourself, Jack?"

"My home is with Amy," replied the boy. "Wherever that is."

"He has no parents either," added Amy.

"Well, Jack, it looks like you will be sharing our house with us," went on Mary. "That is, if Amy will let me stay here. Amy, this house was bought with money your parents left to my brother for you. Since he died the house is yours now. I've been waiting for you to come back. I have no home myself—only a son who is travelling the world."

Amy and Jack flashed a glance at each other.

"Will you let me stay?" repeated Mary. "You will need someone to look after you. As you see I've already made some changes to the place."

"Aunt Mary," replied Amy sincerely, "I feel as if I've known you for a long time. I want you to stay, and I want to stay with you. I'm glad my uncle's gone, but so much more has happened than that, I could hardly begin to tell you."

Mary nodded slowly.

"You can tell me about it when you are ready," she said. "Or if you prefer to say nothing that is also all right. Now will you and Jack come in and share some breakfast with me?"

"Oh yes!" said Amy, for although they had feasted royally with the White Rider, the meal belonged to another world, and in this one—they were hungry again.

The trail ends here. For Jack and Mary and Amy flung open all the doors and windows of her uncle's—Amy's—house and allowed the sweet breezes of the forest to enter in. Many a song that Amy had sung from her casement window returned to her now on the moonlight or in the strong rays of the sun. Jack's verses and poems and stories grew to fill not just one book but many. The place settings of cutlery which they had used to dine with the White Rider—and which they had brought with them—were brought out to share a meal whenever a visitor came to their home. The single goblet—the cup of gold—appeared on their table at special times and, as Jack and Amy looked into it, they remembered all the people who needed and longed for the essence it contained, the rose-scented oil which had awakened Amy.

Many times Miter went back to the old 'house'—the shelter at the foot of the leafy lane. He looked down through the skylight, whose lid Jack drew aside for him, and pressed in his muzzle expecting to find, forever and a day, the White Rider in the galley of his ship.

"Come away, dog, come away," Jack would say at last, and the pair of them would return to Amy, where she waited with the wise horse Daybreak.

Ranald Macdonald was born in Edinburgh in 1955. He was educated at the Edinburgh Academy and at the Rudolf Steiner School. He studied at Aberdeen University, Emerson College in Sussex and the Chrysalis Theatre Acting School in London. He has had two periods of teaching in Steiner/Waldorf Education. Ranald has been a publishing poet and author since his twenties. In poetry, drama and storytelling he has tried to combine the different insights he has received through his background and training. He has received awards from the Arts Councils of Scotland and Northern Ireland. He is the father of four children and stepfather of three. He currently lives with his two sons in Kilkenny, Ireland.